*Also by Fay Weldon*

# FAY WELDON

# THE FAT WOMAN'S JOKE

Flamingo

*An Imprint of HarperCollinsPublishers*

Flamingo
An Imprint of HarperCollins*Publishers*
77–85 Fulham Palace Road,
Hammersmith, London W6 8JB

Flamingo® is a registered trademark of
HarperCollins*Publishers* Ltd

www.fireandwater.com

Published by Flamingo 2003
9 8 7 6 5 4 3 2 1

First published in Great Britain by
Hodder and Stoughton Ltd 1967
First published in paperback by Coronet,
an imprint of Hodder and Stoughton Ltd 1982
Sceptre edition 1993

This novel is a work of fiction.
The names, characters and incidents portrayed in it are
the work of the author's imagination. Any resemblance to
actual persons, living or dead, events or localities, is
entirely coincidental.

ISBN 0 00 710922 9

Set in Garamond 3 by
Rowland Phototypesetting Ltd,
Bury St Edmunds, Suffolk

Printed and bound in Great Britain by
Clays Ltd, St Ives plc

# THE FAT WOMAN'S JOKE

# 1

What Esther Sussman liked about Earls Court was that she didn't know anyone who lived there. The legs which passed the bars of her basement window, day and night, belonged to nobody she had ever seen or would ever have to see again. Between four and six every morning the street would empty, and then the silence would disturb her, and she would wake, and get up, and make herself a cup of cocoa and eat a piece of chocolate cake, icing first. There is nothing, she would think, more delicious than the icing of bought chocolate cake, eaten in the silence and privacy of the night.

During the day she would read science fiction novels. In the evenings she watched television. And she ate, and ate, and drank, and ate.

She ate frozen chips and peas and hamburgers, and sliced bread with bought jam and fishpaste, and baked beans and instant puddings, and tinned porridge and tinned suet pudding, and cakes and biscuits from packets. She drank sweet coffee, sweet tea, sweet cocoa and sweet sherry.

This is the only proper holiday, she thought, that I have had for years; and then she thought, but this is not a holiday, this is my life until I die; and then she would eat a biscuit, or make a piece of toast, and melt some ready-sliced cheese on top of it, remembering that the act of cooking had once been almost as absorbing as the act of eating.

The flat was dark and damp, as was only right and fitting, and the furniture was nailed to the floor in case some passing tenant saw fit to sell or burn it. Esther, in fact, found it pleasant to have her whereabouts controlled by a dozen nails. The less freedom of choice she had the better. She had not felt so secure since she spent her days in a pram.

She lived in this manner for several weeks. From time to time she would put on an old black coat over her old black dress and go to Smith's for more science fiction paperbacks, and to the supermarket for more food. When the cupboards were full of food she felt pleased. When her stocks ran low she became uneasy.

Phyllis was the last of Esther's circle to seek her out. She came tripping prettily down the steps one afternoon; thirty-one and finely boned, beautifully dressed in a red tiny-flowered trouser suit with hat to match – neat, sexy and rich; invincibly lively and invincibly stupid.

She dusted off the seat of the armchair before she sat down. She took off her hat and laid it on the table. She stared sadly at Esther with her round silly eyes; Esther kept her own lowered, and sliced a round of hot buttered toast into fingers. When drops of butter fell on to her black dress she rubbed them in with her hand.

'Oh Esther,' said Phyllis, 'why didn't you tell me? If I had known you'd needed help, I would have been here at once. If you'd left your address —'

'I don't need help. What sort of help should I need?'

'Going off like that without a word to anyone. I thought we were supposed to be friends? Now what are friends for if not for help at times like these?'

'Times like what?' Butter ran down Esther's chin. She salvaged it with her tongue.

'It took me weeks finding you, and you know how busy I am. I tried to make Alan tell me where you were but he just wouldn't, and your lawyer didn't know a thing, and your mother was fantastically evasive, and in the end I ran into Peter and he told me. Do you think that girlfriend of his is suitable? I mean, really suitable? She treats him like dirt. He's too young to know how to cope. I wish you'd stop eating, Esther, you'll be like a balloon.'

Esther surveyed her plump hands and wrists and laughed. It was a grimy flat, and the butter mingled with the dirt round her nails.

'Are you sure you wouldn't like some toast, Phyllis? Toast is one of the triumphs of our civilisation. It must be made with very fresh bread, thickly cut; then toasted very quickly and buttered at once, so the butter is half-melted. Unsalted butter, of course; you sprinkle it with salt afterwards. Sea salt, preferably.'

Esther found to her surprise she was crying. She wiped her face with the back of her hand, smearing a streak of oily grime across her cheek, where the white fat lay thickly larded beneath the skin.

'No thank you. No toast. And that lovely boy Peter. He needs you at this crisis of his life. If ever a boy needed his mother, it's Peter at this moment. And what about poor Alan? It breaks my heart to see all this senseless misery. I don't understand any of it. Your lovely marriage, all in ruins.'

'Marriage is too strong an institution for me,' said Esther. 'It is altogether too heavy and powerful.' And indeed at that moment she felt it to be a single steady crushing weight, on top of which bore down the entire human edifice of city and state, learning and religion, commerce and law; pomp, passion and reproduction besides. Beneath this mighty structure the little needles of feeling which flickered between Alan and her were dreadful in their implication. When she challenged her husband, she challenged her known universe.

'What an odd thing to say. Marriage to me is a source of strength, not a weight upon me. I'm sure that's how one ought to look at it. And you are going back to Alan, aren't you? Please say you are.'

'No. This is my home now. I like it. Nothing happens here. I know what to expect from one day to the next. I can control everything, and I can eat. I like eating. Were I attracted to men, or indeed attractive to them, I would perhaps find a similar pleasure in some form of sexual activity. But as it is, I just eat. When you eat, you get fat, and that's all. There are

4

no complications. But husbands, children — no, Phyllis, I am sorry. I am not strong enough for them.'

'You are behaving so oddly. Have you seen a doctor? I know this divine man in Wimpole Street. He's done marvels for me.'

'I wish you would have something to eat, Phyllis. It makes me nervous, to see you just sitting there, not eating, staring, understanding only about a quarter of what I say.

'I suppose you really do believe that your happiness is consequent upon your size? That an inch or two one way or the other would make you truly loved? Equating prettiness with sexuality, and sexuality with happiness? It is a very debased view of femininity you take, Phyllis. It would be excusable in a sixteen-year-old — if my nose were a different shape, if my bosom were larger, if my freckles were gone, then the whole world would be different. But in a woman of your age it is vulgar.'

'I am sorry, but I see it differently. It is just common-sense to make the most of oneself. In any case, everything is different for you. You don't seem to have to follow the rules, as the rest of us do. To be frank, you are an appalling sight at this very moment; you have let yourself go — but I have known you look quite ravishing. I think Gerry always rather fancied you. And I will say this for Gerry, he has good taste. Otherwise the humiliation would be unendurable. Yet it's odd; they are always women of a totally different type from me. Why do you think that is?'

Esther rose from her chair, her flesh unfolding beneath the loose fabric of her dress. She crossed to the cupboard and presently selected a tin of condensed mushroom soup which she opened, poured into a saucepan, and heated on the stove. Phyllis talked to her friend's broad back like a humming-bird chirping away at a rhinoceros.

'I don't mind about Gerry's fancies, really. It's a very small part of marriage, isn't it? If there's anything I've learned in my life it's that one comes to terms with this kind of thing in the end.'

'I come to terms with nothing.'

'Besides, it's probably just all talk with him. They do say that the men who talk most, do least.'

'They'll say anything to comfort themselves.'

'Oh.' Phyllis abandoned the subject. 'Esther, I don't understand what went wrong between you and Alan, so suddenly. Why are you living down here in this horrible place? And why did *you* leave, not him? I don't believe he turned you out. He's such a good man. He's not impetuous, like Gerry. You always seemed so right for each other, so settled and content. He never even talked about other women, not when you were in the room anyway. Sometimes after I'd been with you both I'd go home and cry because Gerry and I could never be close like you and Alan. The only time Gerry and I are ever close is when we're in bed, and even then I don't really enjoy it. It just seems the most important thing in the world. Can you understand that? And now that you two have split up, it just seems like the end of the world to me. Everything has suddenly become frightening. Esther, you've made me afraid.'

'You are right to feel afraid. Are you sure you don't want some of this soup? It is very good — although perhaps a little salty. That's the trouble with condensed soups. You have to choose between having them too weak or too salty.'

'Why am I right to feel afraid, Esther? What is there to be afraid of? I think and think but I can't make it out. You make me feel all kinds of things are going on underneath which I don't understand. It can't be Gerry, because I know he'll never leave me. He'll just go on having sordid affairs with sordid women, but they mean nothing to him. He tells me so, all the time. He's a hot-blooded man, you see, so it's understandable. It's just something a woman like me has to learn to put up with. And in a way, I suppose it has its advantages. He couldn't blame me if I did look round for my amusements, could he?'

'He would, though.'

'Well it wouldn't be reasonable of him — of course he's not a very reasonable person. That's why I love him. If only I could find an attractive man I'd have a lovely passionate affair with him. But there aren't any attractive men left. Why do you think that is? Esther, you haven't answered my question. Why do you think I am right to feel afraid?'

'Because you are growing old. Because lurking somewhere beneath the surface of your brain is a vision of loneliness, and it will be a terrible moment when it breaks through, and you realise that your future is not green pastures, but the knackers yard. We are all separate people, and we are all alone. It is a ridiculous thing to say that no man is an island. We are all islands. You can die, and Gerry won't. Gerry can die, and you

7

won't. Our lives just go on, separate as they have always been. There are no end of things you can be afraid of, if you put your mind to it. Do have some soup. If I emptied a tin of cream in it might improve matters. And a little tomato sauce would cover up the tinny taste.'

'You say the most terrible things and then you expect me to eat.'

'Of course. You can't put off being useless and old and unwanted for ever. Soon, little Phyllis, you will stop painting your toe-nails. Already I suspect you no longer wear your best knickers to parties. It will all be over for you as it is for me, and love and motherhood and romance will be no more than dreams remembered, and rather bad dreams at that. Your real life will begin as mine has now. This is what it's like. Food. Drink. Sleep. Books. They are all drugs. None are as effective as sex, but they are calmer and safer. Nuts?'

'Nuts? Who? Oh — I see.'

Esther was offering Phyllis a bowl of nuts.

'Nuts are lovely,' said Esther. 'Your teeth go through the middle, and they're white and pure and clean inside, and slightly salty and dirty and sexy outside. They make your mouth just a little sore, so you have to take another mouthful to find out if they really do or not.'

'Esther, if you eat so much you will make yourself ill. You've gone completely to pieces. You must make an effort to pull yourself together. You will have to go on a diet again. You and Alan were on a diet just before all this started. I never thought you'd go through with it, but you did, and I respect you for it. But now you've undone all the good you did.'

Esther looked at Phyllis with distaste. 'Oh go away!' She loomed over Phyllis, dirty-nailed, dirty-faced, brilliant-eyed and dangerous. 'Go away! I didn't want you to come here, asking questions, nagging. I came here to have some peace. I don't want to see anyone. What do you want from me?'

'I want to help you.'

'Don't be so stupid. You help me? You're like a mad old woman battering at the prison gates when the hanging's due. All you really want is just to be in there watching. There's nothing here to watch. Just a fat woman eating. That's all. You can see them in any café, any day. They're all around.'

'You are very upset, Esther,' said Phyllis doggedly. 'I'm your friend. I'm very hurt you didn't turn to me when you were in trouble.'

Esther beat her head with her hand.

'That's what I mean! *"I'm very hurt!"* I can't stand it. What am I supposed to do now? Comfort your stupid little worries? What do you think it all is — some kind of game? This is our life, and it's the only one we're ever going to get, and it's a desperate business, and you come bleating to me about your being hurt because I, being near to death and madness, don't come bleating to you with — oh, he treats me so badly, oh, you know what he said, you know what he did — as if talking can make things different. Phyllis, will you please, for your own sake, go away and leave me alone?'

'No.'

Esther gave up.

'Then I will tell you all about it. And when you have drunk your fill of miseries, perhaps then you will feel satisfied and go away. I warn you, it will not be pleasant. You will become upset and angry. It is a story of patterns but no endings, meanings but no answers, and jokes where it would be nice if no jokes were. You have never heard a tale quite like this before and that in itself you will find hard to endure. Are you sitting comfortably?'

'Yes,' said Phyllis, putting her hands neatly together in her lap.

'Then I'll begin.'

Meanwhile, up in Hampstead, in an attic flat, two other women were talking. There was Susan, who was twenty-four, and Brenda, who was twenty-two. It was Susan's flat, and Brenda was staying in the absence of Susan's boyfriend. Just now Susan was painting a picture of Brenda: these days when she came home from the office she would put on a dun-coloured smock and take up her brush at once. She said it gave her life meaning.

Susan was tall, and slim to the point of gauntness. She had straight very thick fair hair, enigmatic slanty green eyes, high cheekbones, a bold nose and an intelligent expression. From time to time, as she worked, she would see herself in the mirror behind Brenda, and would like what she saw.

'It's a pity,' she said to Brenda, 'that your legs are so heavy. Otherwise you'd stop the traffic in the streets.'

Brenda had long legs and they were, in truth, fairly massive around the thighs. But seen sideways on she was almost as slim as Susan herself. She had a round face and an innocent look. She thought Susan lived a wild, fascinating, exciting life.

'What can I do about my legs?'

'Don't wear trousers,' said Susan.

'But trousers are no bother.'

'You're supposed to bother. You've got to bother if you're a woman. Otherwise you might as well be a man.'

'It's not fair. I didn't ask to be born with legs like pillars.'

'I daresay they are good for child-bearing.'

'Can I look?' Brenda lived in hope that one day Susan would paint a flattering portrait of her. Susan never did.

The telephone rang.

'You'd better answer it,' said Susan. 'If it's Alan I'm not at home. I've gone away for a month to the country.'

It wasn't Alan, but a wrong number.

'Perhaps you should ring him,' ventured Brenda. 'Then you wouldn't be so edgy.'

'I'm not edgy,' said Susan. 'I am upset. So we're all upset. Loving *is* upsetting. That's the point of it.'

'What about his wife? Is she upset?'

'I don't think she feels very much at all. Like fish feel no pain when you catch them. From what Alan says, her emotional extremities are primitive.'

'If I went out with a married man I'd feel awful,' said Brenda.

'Why?'

'I'd worry about his wife.'

'You are very different from me. You are fundamentally on the side of wives, and families. I don't like wives, on principle. I like to feel that any husband would prefer me to his wife. Wives are a dull, dreadful, boring, possessive lot by virtue of their state. I am all for sexual free enterprise. Let the best woman win.'

'If you were married,' said Brenda, 'you would not talk like that.'

'If I was married,' said Susan, 'which heaven forbid, I would make sure I outshone every other woman in the world. I wouldn't let myself go.'

12

'Alan didn't seem your type at all.'

'I don't have a type. You are very vulgar sometimes. You know nothing about sex or art or anything.'

'I don't know why you always want to paint me, then. You seem to have such a low opinion of me. It is very tiring.'

'You have a marvellous face,' said Susan. 'If only you would *do* something with it.'

'What do you mean, do something with it?'

'Give it a kind of style, or put an expression on it that suited it.'

'What would suit it?' Brenda was worried.

'I don't know. I'm getting very bored. Shall we go to the pub?'

'I don't like sitting about in pubs. All those smelly people, so full of drink they don't know what they're doing. Last time I was in a pub a man pee-ed himself, he was so drunk. How can you *talk* to anyone in a pub?'

'You go to pubs to enjoy yourself, not to talk. Communication is on a different level altogether. Sometimes I think you should run home to Mummy. You have no gift for living.'

'Oh all right, we'll go to the pub. But will you tell me all about Alan?'

'What about him? What do you want to know? You are very prurient.'

'I don't want to know all about that. I want to know what you *felt*. You make me feel so outclassed. Your relationships are so major, somehow. Nothing like that ever happens to me.'

'He was on a diet,' said Susan. 'That's a feminine kind of thing to be, really. On the whole masculine things are boring and feminine things are interesting.'

'Men don't bore me,' said Brenda. 'Everything else, but I've never been *bored* by a man.'

'Then you're lucky. But that wasn't what I was saying. You are very dim sometimes.'

Susan took off her smock. Brenda put on her shoes.

'You never know with men,' said Susan, pulling on an open lace-work dress over a flesh-coloured body stocking. 'The ones who are most interesting before, are often the most boring afterwards, and vice versa.'

'In that case,' said Brenda, 'it would be absurd for a girl to marry a man she hadn't been to bed with, wouldn't it? Think of all those poor lovesick virgins in the past, all going starry-eyed to the altar and all destined for a lifetime's boredom. How terrible! And to think that my mother would wish to perpetuate such a system for ever!'

'All human activity,' remarked Susan, painting a rim of black around her eyes, 'is fairly absurd.'

14

Brenda put on her jockey's cap and they left. They were a ravishing pair. People stared after them.

Esther had a very pretty soft voice. It was one of the things that had first made Alan notice her. Now, as she recounted her tale, it floated so meekly out of her lips that it was quite an effort for Phyllis to catch what she was saying.

'Alan and I were accustomed to eating a great deal, of course. We all have our cushions against reality: we all have to have our little treats to look forward to. With Gerry it's looking forward to laying girls, and with you it's looking forward to enduring it, and with Alan and me it was eating food. So you can imagine how vulnerable a diet made us.'

'I wish you would stop using the past tense about you and Alan.'

'I know it is only four weeks ago but it might as well be forty years. My marriage with Alan is over. Please don't interrupt. I am explaining how food set the pattern of our days. All day in his grand office Alan would sip coffee and nibble biscuits and plan his canteen dockets and organise cold chicken and salad and wine for working lunches, and all day at home I would plan food, and buy food, and cook food, and serve food, and nibble and taste and stir and experiment and make sweeties and goodies and tasties for Alan to try out when he came home. I would feel cheated if we were asked out to dinner. I would spend the entire afternoon making myself as beautiful as my increasing age and girth would allow, but still I felt cheated.'

15

'You were a wonderful cook. Gerry used to say you were the best cook in England. When you two came to dinner I would go mad with worry. It would take me the whole day just producing something I wouldn't be ashamed of. And even then I usually was.'

'People who can't cook shouldn't try. It is a gift which you are either born with or you aren't. I used to quite enjoy coming to visit you two in spite of the food. You and Gerry would quarrel and bicker, and get at each other in subtle and not so subtle ways, and Alan and I would sit back, lulled by our full bellies into a sense of security, and really believe ourselves to be happy, content and well-matched. This day, four weeks ago, I really think I thought I was happy. There were little grey clouds, here and there, like Alan's writing, which was distracting him from his job, and Peter's precocity, and my boredom with the house and simply, I suppose growing older and fatter. In truth of course, they weren't little clouds at all. They were raging bloody crashing thunderstorms. But there is none so blind as those who are too stuffed full of food to see.'

'I don't really know what you are talking about.'

'You will come to understand, if you pay attention. You are sure you want me to go on with this story?'

'Yes. Oh Esther, you can't still be hungry!' Esther was taking frozen fish fingers from their pack.

'I have no intention, ever again, of doing without what I want. That was what Alan and I presumed to think we could

16

do, that evening in your house when we decided to go on a diet.'


Phyllis Frazer's living-room was rich, uncluttered, pale, tidy and serene. Yet its tidiness, when the Sussmans arrived, seemed deceitful, and its serenity a fraud. And the Frazers, like their room, had an air of urbanity which was not quite believable. Phyllis's cheeks were too pink and Gerry's smile too wide. The doorbell, Esther assumed, had put a stop to a scene of either passion or rage. Gerry was a vigorous, noisy man, twice Phyllis's size. He was a successful civil engineer.

'I hope we're not early,' said Esther. 'We had to come by taxi. We have this new car, you see.' She was kissed first by Phyllis and then by Gerry, who took longer over the embrace than was necessary. Alan pecked Phyllis discreetly, and not without embarrassment, and shook hands with Gerry. When they sat down for their pre-dinner drinks Gerry could see the flesh of Esther's thighs swelling over the tops of her stockings. Esther was aware of this but did nothing about it. She looked, this evening, both monumental and magnificent. Her bright eyes flashed and her pale, large face was animated. Beside her, Alan appeared insignificant, although when he was away from her he stood out as a reasonably sized, reasonably endowed man. He had a thin, clever, craggy face and an urbane manner. His paunch sat uneasily on a frame not designed for it. He had worked in the same advertising agency for fifteen years, and was now in a position of trust and accorded much automatic respect. His title was 'Executive Creative Controller'.

17

'I know nothing about the insides of cars,' he now said, 'except that whenever I buy a new one it goes for a day and then stops. After that it's garages and guarantees and trouble until I wish I had bought a bicycle instead. I don't even know why I buy cars. It just seems to happen. I think perhaps I was sold this one by one of my own advertisements. I am a suggestible person.'

'You take things calmly,' said Gerry. 'If I bought a car which so much as faltered somebody's head would roll.'

'But you are a man of passions. I am a cerebral creature.'

'It's the British workman,' said Gerry. 'No amount of good design these days can counteract the criminal imbecility of the average British worker.'

'Oh please Gerry darling,' cried his wife. 'No! My heart sinks when I hear those terrible words "these days" and "British workman". I know it is going on for a full hour.'

'A man buys a new car. It costs a lot of money. If it breaks down it is only courtesy to give the matter a little attention, Phyllis.'

He was pouring everyone extremely large drinks – everyone, that is, except his wife.

'What about me?' she piped, trembling. 'I'se dry.'

Grudgingly he poured her a small drink, as a husband might pour one for an alcoholic wife. Phyllis very rarely drank to excess. For every bottle of Scotch her husband drank she would sip an inch or so of gin, on the principle that it would make her monthly period, which frequently bothered her, easier.

'All this talk of cars,' she said, emboldened by his kindness to her, 'I hate it. Don't you Esther? It's such a bore.'

'If you spend enough money on something, you can't afford to think it's a bore.'

'Your wife,' said Gerry, with a disparaging look towards his own, 'is a highly intelligent woman.'

Esther wriggled, showing a little more thigh for his benefit. They all drank rather deeply.

'Sometimes,' said Alan, 'I am afraid that Esther knows everything. At other times I am afraid she doesn't.'

'Why? Are you hiding something from her?' asked Phyllis.

'I have nothing to hide from my Esther.'

'You hide your writing from me. Or try to. You lock it away.'

'Writing?' they cried. 'Writing?'

'Alan has been writing a novel in secret. He sent it off to an agent last week. Now we wait. It makes him bad-tempered. Don't ask me what it's about.'

'What's it like? Are we in it?'

'No,' said Alan shortly. 'You are not.'

'He's the only one who's in it,' said Esther.

'How do you know?' he turned on her, fiercely.

'I was only guessing,' she said. 'Or working from first principles. Why? Are you?'

He did not reply, and presently they lost interest. Phyllis enquired brightly about Peter.

'He can't concentrate on his school work,' said Esther. 'His sex life is too complicated. But I don't think it makes any difference. He was born to pass exams and captain cricket teams. Failure is simply not in his nature.'

'Peter sails unafraid and uncomplicated through life,' said Alan. 'We take little notice of him, and he takes none of us.'

'Shall we eat,' said Phyllis, who appreciated Peter as a boy but not as a son.

'We're still drinking,' said her husband. 'Give us a moment's peace.'

'I'm afraid the beef will be overcooked.'

'Beef is sacred,' said Alan, so they went in to the dining-room, where the William Morris wallpaper contrasted prettily with the plain black of the tablecloth and the white of the Rosenthal china.

They sat around the table.

'Alan can't stand grey beef. He likes it to be red and bloody in the middle. He goes rather far, I think, towards the naked, unashamed flesh. But there we are. Beef is a matter of taste, not absolute values. At least I hope so.'

'Anyway, Gerry thinks if I cook something it is awful, and if you cook something it's lovely, Esther, so why bother.'

'I think you are a superb cook, Phyllis,' lied Esther.

'Or we wouldn't come here,' said Alan.

'Personally, in this house I would rather drink than eat any day,' said Gerry.

'I wish you would stop being horrid to your wife, Gerry,' said Esther, finally coming down on Phyllis's side. 'It makes her cross and everyone's gastric juices go sour. Why don't you just *appreciate* her?'

'She's quite right,' said Alan. 'Women are what their husbands expect them to be; no more and no less. The more you flatter them the more they thrive.'

'On lies?' enquired Gerry.

'If need be.'

Esther was disturbed. 'You are horrible,' she said. 'Can't we just get on with dinner?'

Phyllis passed the mayonnaise, where artichoke hearts, flaked fish, olives and eggs lay immersed. The mayonnaise was perhaps too thin and too salty. They helped themselves, with all the appearance of enthusiasm.

'It has been a hard day,' said Gerry mournfully.

'But rewarding?'

'A new office block to do, if I'm lucky. A new world to conquer.'

'And a new secretary,' said his wife. 'A luscious child, at least eighteen, and nubile for the last five years. Plump, biteable and ripe.'

'Alan has a new secretary,' said Esther. 'I don't know what she looks like. What does she look like, Alan? There she sits, day after day, part of your life but not of mine.' Her voice was wistful.

'She is slim like a willow. But she has curves here and there.' The appreciation in her husband's voice was not at all what Esther had bargained for.

'Oh dear. And I'm so fat. No thanks, Phyllis darling, no more.'

'I like you fat. I accept you fat. You are fat.'

'Not too fat?'

'Well perhaps,' said Alan, 'just a little too fat.'

'Oh,' moaned Esther, taken aback.

'What's the matter now?'

'You've never said that to me before.'

'You've never been as fat as this before.'

'I'm so thin,' complained Phyllis politely, 'I can't get fat. Do you like garlic bread?'

'Superb.'

'Well you can't spoil that, at least,' said Gerry.

'More, Alan?'

'Thank you.'

'Do you think you should?' asked Esther. 'Every time I sew your jacket buttons on I have to use stronger and stronger thread.'

'I admit your point. I am fat too. We are a horrid gross lot.'

'Eat, drink and fornicate,' boomed their host. 'There is too much abstinence going on.' His wife made apologetic faces at the guests.

'If you are fat you die sooner,' said Alan.

'Who cares?' asked his wife, but no one took any notice, so

she said, 'Tell me about your secretary, Alan. Besides being so slim, but curvacious with it, what is she like? Perhaps you wish she was me?'

'What is the matter with you?'

'It's us,' said Phyllis dismally. 'Discontent is catching.'

'I am not discontented. I just hope Alan isn't. Who am I to compete with a secretary fresh from a charm school, with a light in her eye and life in her loins?'

'Careful, Esther,' said Gerry. 'Those are Phil's lines, to be spoken in a plaintive female whine and guaranteed to drive a man straight into a mistress's arms.'

'One wonders which comes first,' she said, 'the mistress or the female whine. It would be interesting to do a study.'

Alan decided to bring the table back to order.

'You have no cause for concern whatsoever, Esther. To tell you the truth I can't even remember her name. It is entirely forgettable. I think it is Susan. She can't type to save herself. She is thin. She is temporary. I think she thinks she is not a typist by nature, but something far more mysterious and significant, but this is a normal delusion of temporary staff. She is in, I imagine, her early twenties. She keeps forgetting that I like plain chocolate biscuits, and dislike milk chocolate biscuits. Now you, Esther, never make mistakes like that. You have a clear notion of what is important in life. Namely money, comfort, food, order and stability.'

'You make me sound just like my mother. Is that what you really think of me?'

'No. I am merely trying to publicly affirm my faith in you, marriage and the established order, and to explain that I am content with my lot. I am a married man and I married of my own free will. I am a city man, and live in the city of my own free will. A company man, also of my own volition. So I should not be surprised to find myself, in middle-age, a middle-aged, married, company, city man – with no power in my muscles and precious little in my mind. Here in this sulphurous city I live and die, with as much peace and comfort as I can draw around me. Work, home, wife, child – this is my life and I am not aggrieved by it. I chose it. I know my place. I daresay I shall die as happy and fulfilled as most.'

'It sounds perfectly horrible to me,' said Esther. 'However, I don't take you seriously because you have just sent your magnum opus to a publisher, and I know you are quite convinced you will spend your declining years in an aura of esteem and respect and creative endeavour. I believe also that somewhere down inside you lurks a rich fantasy life in which you travel to exotic places, conquer mountains, do any number of noble and heroic deeds, save battalions singlehanded, and lay the world's most beautiful women right and left. There may well be a more perverse and morbid side to this, but I would rather not go into it here. And you, Gerry, tell me, do *you* not ever wish to do extreme and fearful things? Is your masculinity entirely channelled into lustful thoughts of the opposite sex? Do you not want to burn, savage, torture, kill? Or at any rate, like Alan, failing that, are you not seized with the desire to break all the best glasses, miss the basin when you pee, burn

25

the sheets with cigarette ends, leave smelly socks about for your wife to pick up –'

'Women have their revenges too –' said Alan. 'They leave old sanitary towels around.'

Abruptly they all stopped talking. Alan crammed more garlic bread into his mouth. He bit upon a garlic clove and was obliged to spit it out. Everyone watched.

'We all talk too much,' said Esther to Phyllis in the kitchen a little later. 'One has to be careful with words. Words turn probabilities into facts, and by sheer force of definition translate tendencies into habits. Our home isn't half going to be messy from now on.'

When they returned to the kitchen with the second course, the murmur of men's voices stopped abruptly.

'What were you telling Alan to do?' Phyllis asked her husband. 'Go off with his secretary? For the sake of his red corpuscles?'

He did not reply, for this indeed had been the essence of his conversation.

'Esther,' was all Alan said, 'we are going on a diet, you and I. We are going to fight back middle-age. Hand in hand, with a stiff upper lip and an aching midriff, we are going to push back the enemy.'

'When?' asked Esther in alarm, looking at the mountains of food on the table – the crackling hot pottery dishes of vegetables, the bowls of sauces, the great oval platter on which the bloody beef reposed. 'Not now?'

'Of course not,' said Alan. 'Tomorrow we start.'

'New lives always begin tomorrow,' said Phyllis. 'Never now. That's right, isn't it, Gerry? Will you carve?'

Gerry sharpened the knife. It flashed to and fro under their noses. He carved.

'We're going to do it, Esther,' said Alan, watching the food piling on her plate. 'Look your last on all things lovely. We'll take a stone off apiece.'

'If you say so, darling,' said Esther. 'I'm all yours to command.'

'Oh she's a lovely woman,' said Gerry.

'You'll never stick it,' said Phyllis, jealously. 'You'll never be able to do it.'

'Of course we will,' said Esther. 'If we want to, we will. And we want to.'

'Doing without what you want is the hardest thing in the world,' said Phyllis. 'Isn't it, Gerry?'

'Incidentally,' said Esther to Phyllis four weeks later, 'there was too much salt in the mayonnaise that night, and too much

27

in the gravy too. So we had to drink a lot. And the next day Alan and I had hangovers, and were cross and miserable even before we started our régime of abstinence.'

'You didn't say anything about too much salt at the time.'

'One doesn't. Or nobody would ever ask anyone to dinner any more. The middle classes would grind to a social halt. It wasn't a bad meal, for once, in fact. Which was just as well, because it was the last we had for some time.'

'After you two had gone,' said Phyllis, 'I went to sleep on the sofa. Gerry wouldn't stop visiting his ex-wife every Saturday, and I was upset and angry, and I thought he'd been behaving badly all evening, anyway. But in the middle of the night he hauled me into bed – he's much stronger than I am – and we were happy for a time. Until Saturday came again. Or at least he was happy. I'm not very good at that kind of thing. It's the gesture I appreciate, not the thing itself. I think.'

'And Alan and I went home and had cocoa and biscuits and went to sleep. We were tired. We'd been married, after all, for nearly twenty years.'

'But you and Alan were always touching each other,' said Phyllis, 'like young lovers. As if even after all those years you couldn't keep your hands off each other.'

'And we meant it,' said Esther crossly, 'in public. It was just when we got home we found we were tired. Once you are beyond a certain age sex isn't an instinct any more – it's a social convention.'

'Speak for yourself.'

'I am sorry, but you feel sexy because you know it's nice to feel sexy, not because you really are. Are you sure you wouldn't like coffee?'

'No,' said Phyllis. Then she added, urgently, 'Esther! Living here, alone, with no husband. No boyfriend. Surely you feel – at night –?'

'No. I live by myself. Just me. Self-sufficient, wanting no one, no other mind, no other body. I live with the truth. I need no protection from it.'

'Gerry and I,' said Phyllis. 'I am so miserable. We are chained together by our bed.'

'That is your misfortune,' said Esther, 'and why you are so unhappy. Bed is a very difficult habit to break. Now let us continue with my story, because yours is very ordinary and I am not concerned with it. In the morning Alan kissed me goodbye – on the doorstep so the neighbours could see – and went to his office. He had had no breakfast. He was feeling desperate and hungover, but dieting seemed to him to be a rich and positive thing. Perhaps that was why, this particular morning, his secretary made such an impression on him, and he on his secretary.'

Susan and Brenda sat in the pub, conscious of their youth and beauty, which indeed shone like a beacon in a boozy, beery world, and Susan gave Brenda her more detailed account of a morning which Esther could only guess at.

'The typing agency quite often send me to Norman, Zo-Hailey –' said Susan, naming a large London advertising agency. 'They always need temporary staff. Girls never stay long. They think it's going to be glamorous and all they find is a lot of dull old research people plodding through statistics. Married ones, at that. And the pay's bad, so they hand in their notice. And then again, if they do get to the livelier departments, it soon transpires that men in advertising agencies hardly count as men. What man worth his salt would spend his life sitting in an office selling other people's goods, by proxy?'

'Alan seems to have behaved like a man, from what you say.'

'Alan was different. He was a creative person. Anyway they're all quite good at pretending to be men. They know all the rules. Their bodies, even, work as if they were men, but on the whole they're deceiving themselves and everyone else.'

'Perhaps you and I are only pretending to be women. How could we tell?'

'We are both flat-chested, it is true,' said Susan, 'and when I come to think of it, Alan had very pronounced nipples at the beginning of that fortnight. Almost what approached a bosom. It fascinated me. I had never encountered anything like it before. I began to wonder if I perhaps had lesbian tendencies.'

'It sounds perfectly revolting.'

'Not in the least. He has this thin face to counteract it. He was an important man at Zo's. Everyone seemed to think I ought to be pleased to work for him but all I did was make rather more mistakes than usual. He never got irritated. He just used to sigh and raise his eyebrows at me as if I was a naughty child but he would forgive me. In the end I began to feel quite like a daughter to him. And when one's father turns lascivious eyes upon one, that's that, isn't it? You get all stirred up inside. You begin to want to impress. You find yourself putting on make-up just to come to work. And he'd written this novel, and his agent rang up and raved about it, and I listened on the extension when I was getting the coffee in the outer office. I find there is something very erotic about literary men, don't you?'

'I really don't know. I haven't been in London long enough. Anyway, I thought you were supposed to be in love with William Macklesfield.' William Macklesfield was the middle-aged poet who had been seen occasionally on the television, and with whom, on and off, Susan had been sleeping for years.

'William and I are very close. We are best friends. We have a wonderful platonic relationship with sex lying, as it were, on top of it. But we are not in love. Not the kind of lightning love which suddenly flashes out of a clear sky and tumbles you on your back.'

'Good heavens,' said Brenda. 'Things like that never happen to me.'

'It's your pillar-like legs,' said Susan. 'And your matriarchal destiny. Your time will come when you are sixty, surrounded by your grandchildren and bullying your sons. When I am an ageing drunken lush only fit for a mental home, then I daresay you will be glad that you are you and I am I. In the meantime I can fairly say that of the two of us, I have the more style.'

'Thank you very much, I'm sure.'

'Unless of course, I compromise, and marry. I might become a poet's wife. But poets I find, are often rather dull. They are in the habit of expressing themselves through the written word, and not through their bodies. William is awful in bed.'

'What *does* that mean?' asked Brenda. 'I thought it was the way a girl responded, not what the man did, that mattered. I never have any trouble. I always thought that girls saying men were bad in bed was just a way of making them feel nervous.'

'Oh you,' said Susan, 'you should write a column in a woman's magazine. I can see it happening yet.'

'You were talking,' said Brenda, devastated, 'about this lightning stroke which flung you back upon your bed with your knees apart.'

'I didn't say with my knees apart. Nor did I mention bed.'

'I thought it was what you meant.'

'You are not at all open to *forces*, are you?' said Susan. 'You are an artifact. You are not swayed by passions like me.

Anyway, there I was, working in this great throbbing organisation, beginning to fancy my boss, and his wife would ring up every day and ask what he wanted for dinner. He would take her so seriously, I couldn't understand it. He would think and ponder, and sometimes he would ring her back later to give her a considered answer. It bespoke such intimacy. It drove me mad. She had such a soft, possessive voice. I wondered why he took so little notice of me. And why was there no one *I* could ring up, in the perfect security of knowing they would be home for dinner, come what may, and obliged to eat what I provided? William kept going back home to his wife for dinner and I found this most irritating. And why didn't Alan's wife ring up and ask him what did he want to do in bed that night, or something? Why was it always dinner? Poor man, I thought. Poor blind man. Here was I, young, clever and creative, with depths to plumb, able to take a constructive interest in what really interested him, sitting docile and waiting at his elbow, typing and all he'd do was let his eyes stray to my legs and back again. He was too busy telling his wife what he wanted for dinner. It was an insult to me. I wanted to ask about his novel but he seemed to want to keep it secret. He was so clever. Not just with words, but he loved painting, too. He used to be a painter before his wife got hold of him and destroyed him with boredom and responsibilities. Domesticity had him trapped. Can you imagine, he even kept family photographs on his desk!'

'A commercial artist, do you mean?'

'No, I do not. He went to art school. He married her very young, on impulse, and had to give up all thought of being a proper painter. She drove him into advertising, and he ended up a kind of co-ordinator of words and pictures. A man with a great deal of power over people of no consequence whatsoever, and a long title on the plate on his door. How bitter! He should never have let her do it to him. Brenda, do stop making eyes at that Siamese gentleman.'

'He is not Siamese, I don't think. But he is very handsome.'

'I wonder why he seems to prefer you to me. Perhaps it's his nationality. Do you want me to go on with this story?'

'Yes.'

'Then try and concentrate. The first time he actually laid hands on me was the day he started his diet, the day he heard from his agent.'

On the first morning of the diet pigeons chose to strut about the windowsill and embarrass Alan with their intimacies. There was a red carpet on the office floor; red curtains at the window. The standard lamp was grey, and so was the upholstery of the armchairs. His desk was large, sleek, new and empty, except for a list of the day's engagements. He earned £6,000 a year and was not quite on the Board. It seemed doubtful, now, that he would ever get there. One younger, more energetic man had already used him as a footstool for a leap to Board level, and once a footstool, in Company terms, nearly always a footstool. And nothing would deter the pigeons.

Susan came in with a tray of coffee and biscuits. She wore a very short white skirt and a skimpy grey jersey.

'Mr Sussman –' said Susan, apologetically. She wore an enormous pair of spectacles. Her eyesight was normal, but the glasses combined frailty of flesh with aggression of spirit, and she enjoyed them. Alan sought for her features behind them. He was flushed after his telephone conversation with his agent.

'I am really very sorry –'

'Oh my God, what have you done now?' He spoke amiably, as well may a man who has just achieved, he thinks, a lifelong ambition.

'It's just that I forgot about your biscuits again. I took the milk chocolate, not the plain. My gentleman friend always prefers milk, and I become confused.'

'Your gentleman friend?'

'How else would you have me describe him? My quasi-husband, my seducer, my lover, my fiancé? Take your pick. He is a poet.'

'It is too unsettled a relationship that you describe,' said Alan, 'for my peace of mind. Secretaries, however temporary, should maintain the illusion of being either virgins or well-married. Otherwise the mind begins to envisage possibilities. The girl takes on flesh and blood. You are a bad secretary.'

'I'm sorry about the biscuits.'

'I was not talking about the biscuits, and well you know it. It does not matter about the biscuits. I am not eating the biscuits.'

'Not eating the biscuits?'

'No. And no sugar in the coffee.'

'No sugar in the coffee?'

'Stop playing the little girl. You are a grown woman. I am on a diet.'

'Oh no!'

'Why not? I'm too fat.'

'People on diets become cross, bad-tempered. And desire fails. You are not too fat. Why do you want to be thin?'

'I want to be young again.'

'Why?'

'Because when I was young I had hopes and aspirations and I liked the feeling.'

'I think you are foolish. You don't have to be young to achieve things. I like an older man myself.'

'You do?'

'Oh yes.'

'All the same, take the biscuits away.'

'I will keep them for William.'

'The poet? I would rather you didn't.'

'Why not?' She took off her glasses to see him better.

'The thought confuses me. It is a relief your glasses have gone. Now I can see your face.'

'It is just a face like any other.'

'It is not. It is a remarkable face. I would like to paint it.'

'I do self-portraits, sometimes.'

'Do you paint?'

'Yes.'

'You're not really a secretary?'

'No.'

'They never are,' he said. 'They never are. All summer in the temporary season, they never are. That's why the typing is so bad. Get on with it.'

Routed, she sat and typed. He sat and read marketing reports and wondered whether to ring Esther and tell her his agent liked the novel. He decided against it. He feared she might prick the bubble of his self-esteem too soon.

'I am not a foolish girl,' said his secretary presently. 'You lead me on in order to make me look silly, but that is easy to do. It's rather cheap of you.'

'Oh good heavens,' Alan said. 'This is an office not a —'

'Not a what?'

'You go too far. You talk like a wife, full of reproaches. I warn you. You are a fantastic creature but you go too far.'

'Fantastic?' Her eyes were bright.

'You are very beautiful, or look so to me this morning.' He came to look over her shoulder, as if to see what she was typing. 'What scent are you wearing?'

'Madam Rochas. It's not too much?'

'Not at all. It is nourishing. Do you know what I had for breakfast? Two boiled eggs and some black coffee. Do you know what I shall have for lunch? Two boiled eggs and a grapefruit. And for dinner an omelette, and some black coffee, and guess what. A tomato.'

'Oh big deal!' she said. 'Do you expect me to be sorry for you?'

'No.' His hands trembling, slid over her breasts. 'I am only

38

explaining that I am light-headed and cannot be held responsible for my actions.'

The telephone rang. It was Esther. Did he want a herb omelet and a tomato, separate, or the tomato cooked in with the omelette? The former, he thought.

'She has a pretty voice,' said Susan. 'Is she pretty?'

But Alan was back at his desk. He seemed to have forgotten the past few minutes entirely. He was formal, brisk and cold.

'Get Andrew to come and see me,' he said, studying a folder of layouts launching a change in the formula of a dandruff shampoo. 'I don't know what is happening to Andrew's judgement.' Susan rang through and presently Andrew, a thin, well-born young man with a double first, came in to be chided. He reminded Alan of himself when young. Susan sulked and plotted.

'It was quite true,' said Susan to Brenda in the pub. 'He was already light-headed, otherwise I might never have got him to the point of touching me, from which all else stemmed. He was used at that hour of the morning to having a stomach full of cereal, eggs and bacon, toast and marmalade, tea, topped up by coffee and biscuits. And all of a sudden there was nothing inside him – only the vision of me, and the words I spun around him. If I spoke boldly, it was because that was what he responded to. He would never seduce, he would have to be seduced. But I trembled inside; it took every ounce of courage I had to speak to him the way I did. And when he touched me –'

'Lightning? You fell back upon the bed?'

'I was in an office, idiot. Had there been a bed, I would have. But he was not quite ready yet to fall on top of me, of course. I had further work to do.'

'I think you're making it all up, talking as if you did it all on purpose. Anyway men aren't manipulated like that. They either feel things for you or they don't. It's men who take the initiative. You keep talking about men the way men talk about women. It's rather disgusting.'

'You put things into their heads,' Susan insisted. 'You put beddish visions before their eyes.'

'I think that's a very old-fashioned view,' said Brenda. 'All this talk of seducing and being seduced. It's not like that at all. Everyone knows exactly what they're doing these days.'

'Well he didn't. He really didn't. He was too hungry for one thing.'

'You're older than me, almost of another generation. I expect that's why you take such an old-fashioned view.'

'You're drunk and you're jealous,' said Susan correctly. 'Let's go home.'

They rose to go. The man who came from the East rose too and followed them out into the street. He was following Brenda, not Susan.

❒

'That morning when I rang and asked about the omelette,' said Esther to Phyllis in the basement, 'his voice sounded odd, and I had this sudden vision of his temporary secretary sitting there exhibiting her legs to him under the desk. He had described her the evening before at your place in altogether too detailed terms for my peace of mind. I was hungry and faint – what with the hangover and the black coffee – quarts of it – and cigarette after cigarette, and I was just standing looking out of the window, which was foolish because Juliet – that's the daily help – was polishing the floor and one shouldn't stand about being idle when other people are working hard. Especially when they're Juliet. Day One of the diet was a horrible day for me; although no doubt it was a delight to my husband.'

Esther's living-room was filled to the point of obsession with Victoriana. Sofas and chairs were buttoned and plump; walls were covered with pictures from ceiling to floor; occasional tables were almost hidden by lamps, clocks, figurines and vases. There was an embroidery frame where it was Esther's habit to sit in the evening, working minute stitches with her puffy hands. Everything in the room was dusted, polished and neat; but this was no thanks to Juliet, who this morning wildly and inefficiently polished the floor. Esther moved away from the window, steering her bulk with grace through the fragile bric-à-brac.

'Juliet,' said Esther, 'you'll never get a good shine if you don't sweep properly first. You'll just rub the dirt in and ruin the surface.'

41

Juliet put down her cloth and straightened up. She was thirty and short, with an hourglass figure and a tendency to backache with which she excused her bad temper.

'Why aren't you in the kitchen?' Juliet's voice was accusing. 'You're always in the kitchen while I polish, cooking.'

'We are on a diet and there's nothing to cook.'

'Well don't take it out on me,' said Juliet, resuming her crouching position and the flailing of her arms.

'I'm not taking anything out on anybody. I'm just observing that if you rub grit into a parquet floor you spoil the surface.'

'The Hoover needs mending,' said Juliet. 'It doesn't take anything up any more. I told you about it weeks ago.'

'Well, you can sweep, can't you? Brooms were made before Hoovers.'

Juliet put down her cloth. 'What did you have for breakfast? Did you go without, or something?'

'I had a very good breakfast, thank you. I had eggs. And it's eggs for lunch, and eggs for dinner, and in two weeks I'll have lost a stone and a half.'

'You be careful. You can go too far. A friend of mine went on a diet and lost all appetite for food. They took her in at the hospital but it was too late, she died. Her stomach had shrunk to a dried pea – or was it walnut? One or the other, I do remember that.'

'This is a very well-tried diet, and very sensible. One should be able to control one's size, if one is going to control one's life.'

'What do you want to do it for? You're all right as you are. You've got a husband and a son and a house, even if it is filled up with all this junk, and someone to do your dirty work for you. What else do you want?'

'It's healthier to be thin.'

'Dieting ruins the health. Men like women nice and cosy. Their wives, anyway.'

'To tell you the truth I am really going through with it for Mr Sussman's sake. For my own part, I don't really worry. But it's easier for him if I do it too. You know what men are. They haven't got all that much willpower.'

'What you need is physical exercise. You ought to get down on your hands and knees more often, instead of just standing about.'

'When you have gone home, Juliet,' said Esther clearly, 'I often find I have to.'

She walked with determination into the kitchen, as if there was something there to busy her. Juliet peered after her, with an expression of quite serious malevolence on her face.

'You'll go too far,' said Juliet. 'One day you'll go too far.'

And she continued her manic, useless polishing.

The Sussmans' kitchen was full of herbs, spices, pestles and mortars and strings of onion and garlic, and jars of olive oil and cut-outs from early editions of Mrs Beeton. There scarcely seemed room in it for human beings, but that evening there they were, the two of them, Alan and Esther, their flesh squeezed between table and dresser, studying their diet sheet, and both bad-tempered.

'At least we can put herbs in the omelette,' said Alan. 'An *omelette aux fines herbes*. Delicious.'

Esther reached out for eggs and started breaking them into a basin. 'Oh big deal,' she said.

'Someone else said that to me today. I can't remember who.'

'Your secretary, I dare say. Since she spends so much time with you.'

'I think it was, now you come to mention it.'

Esther was suspicious. It did not suit her. Her eyes, usually luminous globes of expression, became smaller and mean. 'What were you and she talking about?'

'This diet, I think,' said Alan, allowing a certain weariness at Esther's bad behaviour to creep into his tone. 'I really can't remember. I've got to talk to somebody, haven't I?'

'This Susan seems to be quite your confidante. Do you discuss all your personal life with her?'

'Not particularly.'

'Do you discuss me?' She used her little-girl voice.

He used his angry one. 'As much, I daresay, as you discuss me with your window cleaner.'

'My window cleaner appears to be quite a randy man, for your information.'

'So, if you want to know, does my secretary.'

'What, a randy man?'

'No, a randy girl. Now you know.'

She chose not to believe him. She thought she had simply made him angrier than she had meant.

'I'm sorry,' she said. 'I'm being silly. It's because I'm hungry.'

'Yes you are being silly. Why are you dividing the whites from the yolks?'

'I'm making a fluffy omelette. It will go further.'

Esther's head, all of a sudden, felt very full and unpleasant. 'I feel awful.'

'I feel fine,' said Alan, with memories of Susan's forwardness and hugging to himself the knowledge of his agent's enthusiasm, which he felt Esther did not yet deserve to know. 'Lighter and emptier. I think this is what it felt like ten years ago.' He looked down at his paunch. It seemed to him to have shrunk.

'I've got a headache. I don't think I can face this omelette.' She laid her hands on her stomach. It was full and flabby. She was depressed.

'It says you must not on any account go without any of the food items mentioned. You just wait until spinach day!' He quoted from the diet sheet. *The diet depends for its efficiency on a chemical process the body undergoes during the diet's course.* They may be good doctors but they're bloody awful writers of the King's English.'

'Queen's.'

'Why do you have this urge to find fault all the time?'

'That's very unfair.'

'What are you doing with that butter?' Alan's hand shot out to restrain Esther's. They both stared at their touching flesh, as if at something strange. Alan dropped her hand, quickly.

'You've got to have butter to make an omelette, silly.'

'It says on the diet sheet no dairy products whatsoever.'

'Don't be stupid.' She sneered quite visibly, her top lip curling over her tiny sharp teeth. 'How can you make an omelette without butter?'

'I don't know, but you've got to!'

'Then *you* do it!' She shouted at him. A glass mobile trembled, and the noise of its tinkling shamed her and pleased him. He seized the omelette mixture and poured it straight into the unbuttered pan. He took up the wooden spoon and scraped it off the bottom. It looked more like scrambled egg than omelette.

'There you see!' she cried, vindicated. 'You've made a mess of it the way you make a mess of everything.'

Alan decided it was time to bring the situation back into his control. 'Esther,' he said, 'either we do this diet or we don't. I think it is important that we should. We would both benefit by losing weight.'

'You mean *I* would. You don't find me attractive any more. You're ashamed to be seen out with me because I'm fat and horrible and you think people will be sorry for you because you're married to me.'

Alan still held the frying pan in his hand. The whites of his eyes glinted in the light from the oil lamp. It seemed for a moment that he was going to throw the omelette full in his wife's face, but at that moment his son, Peter, came into the room, and he lowered the pan and rearranged his face into a less manic pattern. Esther for her part stopped cowering, straightened up and smiled maternally.

47

Peter was six foot two, some six inches taller than his father. He was pink-faced, blond, well-built and gave an immediate impression of health and cheerfulness. Otherwise he was very like his father. The school uniform he was obliged to wear did not succeed in making him look like a child.

'You two squabbling?' He strode to the refrigerator, plucked it open, and peered inside. 'Can I make myself some sausages and bacon? And fried bread?'

'You'll get fat,' said his mother.

'Not me. I've got youth on my side.'

'Your heredity's working against you, don't forget that,' said Alan, meaning Esther.

'You should learn dietary discipline now,' she said, 'so in the future you will be able to control your weight at will.'

'Hark who's talking. Really, Mum!'

'I'm sure I hope my children will do better than I. Because I am morally frail and weak-willed, this is no reason for you to be content to be the same. There is no possible point in procreation if one's children do not outstrip one in every respect. Put the bread away. Fried bread is going too far.'

'Why don't you two sit down and eat that omelette? You'd feel much better.'

They obeyed.

'Why is it,' he asked, as the smell of frying bacon filled the room, 'that people who are quite wilfully spoiling their own enjoyment cannot rest there but are also obsessively anxious to spoil other people's? "Put the bread away", indeed!'

'Stop trying to talk like your mother,' said Alan, scraping the last scrap of egg from his plate, adding, 'There's a very odd smell in here.'

'I can smell it too,' Esther had already finished and now sat, desolately, with her knife and fork neatly together on her bare plate. She turned her head like a questing dog, sniffing.

'It's the bacon,' said Peter. 'Incidentally, it is very thinly cut bacon. Why can't we get it thicker?'

'Because thin bacon is an excellent economy. It is the one economy I have. It's not the smell of bacon, I can assure you.'

'Oh of course,' said Peter. 'I forgot. It's aniseed.'

'Aniseed?'

'Aniseed?'

'From the buns. We're filling buns with aniseed. Then you throw them at the patrol dogs and they go after the buns, and not you.'

'Patrol dogs?'

'I could do with some more sausages.'

'Patrol dogs?' Alan's normally pale face was pink. As his colour heightened the resemblance between him and his son became more apparent.

'Down at Frampton. There's a biological warfare place down there. We're going down on a demo.'

'We?'

'Stephanie and me.'

'Stephanie?'

'You know Stephanie.' Another mouthful, and another bacon rasher disappeared. His parents watched.

'The one with the hair?'

'It's easier to look after like that. Cropped.'

'She could shave it right off and polish the skin,' said Esther. 'Then she could seal it, to preserve the shine.'

'That was not worthy of you, Mother.'

'I'm sorry,' she said, humbly, 'I am not at my best when hungry, and your father keeps getting at me –' Alan took out his cigarettes and failed to offer her one – 'but she's a very nice girl, I know, and extremely bright. I like her. I understand she is very popular.'

'It is true,' said Peter nobly, 'that she does sometimes get mistaken for a boy, by the older generation. Never our own, however, and that is the most important thing. I do realise it is hard for people of your age to adjust yourselves to current values, and I appreciate the effort you both make. I mean really.'

'Tell me more about the patrol dogs,' said Alan.

'I don't like people who organise diseases for the benefit of humanity. I mean, do you? The least I feel I can do is register my protest. So I shall sit down on the ground in a field along with a couple of hundred others, until shifted by some force other than my own.'

'Oh youth, youth!' said Alan, not altogether displeased. 'What good do you think it will do?'

'I don't know. None, probably. I don't much care. It will make me feel better,' Peter rose and cut himself a thick slice of bread. He spread it with butter, and covered it with apricot jam in which the apricots lay sugary and whole. 'Well I mean,' he went on, as his teeth slipped through the soft slice, 'you two went on marches once, didn't you? And left-wing meetings? You waved banners, along with the rest. You helped save the world. The world's the same as it always was, but what happened to you when you stopped trying to save it?'

'All that was a long time ago,' said Alan. 'Thank God.'

'We grew up,' said Esther. 'We gained a sense of reality.'

'You grew fat and cosy and comfortable, you mean,' said Peter. 'You changed sides, that's what happened to you!'

51

Esther jumped to her feet: she all but shouted. 'I am not fat and cosy and comfortable. Neither is Alan.'

'Oh Mum!' he said reproachfully, from his great rosy height. 'Oh Dad! Look at yourselves.'

Esther sat down again. Her heavy breasts drooped over the table. His paunch swelled beneath its top.

'I'm sorry I tried to cook that omelette in butter,' she said presently. 'It was stupid of me.'

'Oh forget it,' said her husband, who had no intention of doing so. 'Cigarette?'

Phyllis, listening to Esther's account of the first day of the diet, was beginning to feel hungry herself. She drank a cup of coffee and accepted a biscuit. 'You'll have to go on a diet again, Esther,' she said nibbling.

'But what's the point? What's the point?' Esther had stopped eating for the moment, and despair now rose up her gullet. 'There is only one virtue these days, and that is to be young. Everything is forgiven to the young – even fatness, and that is saying something. And I am no longer young. Nothing will be forgiven me. All I can hope is not to be noticed any more.'

'You're talking nonsense,' said Phyllis. 'You're just depressed. I know some very pretty and very elegant elderly ladies indeed. Most charming.'

'Har, har, har,' said Esther. 'And men laugh at them behind their backs for being old, in just the same spirit as men will laugh at girls with no ankles, and girls with spots, and girls with bad breath, because for all their efforts they fail to please. There's more dignity, if one is neither young nor beautiful, in simply giving up. Which is what, being middle-aged, I am finally allowed to do.'

'I think the way you sit and guzzle is most undignified. I think you should have more pride in yourself. It's your own opinion of yourself that counts, not other people's.'

'Oh Miss Smarmy,' said Esther. 'I was telling you a story. If you don't want to hear it, go away.'

'Oh please go on. You haven't told me anything yet, really.'

'There are many things I want you to understand first. One of the terrible things about marriage is the dread of change that goes with it, as perhaps even you are aware in your own relationship with Gerry. Any change, and you begin to worry. Either Alan wanted me to be thin because he was fancying his secretary, or he wanted me to be thin because he was ashamed of me the way I was. Either way, he wanted me to be different from what I was, and this to me seemed the most devastating insult.'

'He'd had secretaries before. Why were you worrying about this one?'

'Her name was Susan. I've never liked girls called Susan. I don't trust them. My mother's second name is Susan.'

'What does your mother say about your not being at home? She adores Alan.'

'I'll come to that later. She's been down here, you know, prying and spying.' Her voice, as always when Esther talked about her mother, became smaller and meaner, like her eyes.

'You're awful about your mother. She's such a wonderful person.'

'Oh yes. Of course. Any woman who gets past sixty is wonderful. I look forward to it, I'm sure. I hope to be dead by then.'

'And to suspect Alan of carrying on with his secretary because her name's the same as your mother's is just plain silly.'

'Well that's the way it goes, doesn't it. I didn't ask you to come down here, making me talk. I'm beginning to feel very upset. I was quite peaceful before. Now I'm all stirred up. I feel sick. I'm getting indigestion.'

'It's jealousy that gives me a pain,' said Phyllis, taking another biscuit. 'First I get the pain, and from that I know I'm jealous. It's down here.'

'Down here! Down here! In your womb, you silly barren bitch.'

'What a horrible thing to say. It's not in my womb, anyway. I know where my womb is. It's higher. I am not barren. Gerry and I simply can't decide whether or not we want children. Or rather, Gerry can't. And you've only got one child; why do you try to make out you're so fertile?'

'I don't. I'm not. I am wounded, through and through. Marriage is such a falling away. It hurts. When you go to the pictures you remember a time you used to hold hands. You go to bed in your curlers and remember a time you used to sleep in each other's arms. Nothing is ever as it was, in marriage.'

'I try to keep our love alive,' said Phyllis, her dolly eyes wide with virtue. 'Gerry's and mine. I wouldn't dream of going to bed in curlers.'

Esther quelled her irritation by unwrapping a chocolate and eating it. It was toffee and she had to speak now through jaws that had trouble in opening.

'Anyway that night we slept as far apart from each other as we could and Alan was late for work, and got closer to Susan as a result.'

'How do you know?'

'Because the more he fancied her the nastier he was to me. That's the way guilt takes him. He loads it on to me. He goads me into behaving badly so then he can consider himself justified. Kick the old nagger in the teeth, and cry "She drove me to it!" in the young one's bed. That's the way it goes.'

'I'm sure it wasn't. I think you're making it all up about Alan. He's very loyal to you. He loves you.'

'Love, shmove,' she said. 'Love, shmove!' and ate the last biscuit on the plate.

❏

'Are you sure you want me to go on with the story?' asked Susan, when the two girls were back in the flat with the young man from abroad. He sat in the best chair sipping a cup of coffee, nodding benignly and watching every move that Brenda made. It was not clear whether or not he spoke English, since he said nothing. Susan was irritated by his presence, but could think of no good reason for objecting to it. 'Perhaps you would prefer me to go out or something, so you and this extraordinary person can be alone.'

'Good heavens no. What are you thinking of?' Brenda seemed surprised.

'Don't you want to get to know him better or something?'

'Not particularly.'

'Then why is he here?'

'Well, he just came, didn't he? It would seem inhospitable to turn him away. He is a stranger in a foreign land, after all.'

'I expect he comes from Bermondsey, if the truth was known. I don't want to go on if he can understand. It is all very personal to me.'

The two girls stared at him. He smiled and nodded, as if he would say something nice if only he knew how.

'Don't be silly,' said Brenda. 'You see! He doesn't understand a word we say. He's just a nice friendly man having a cup of coffee in a foreign land.'

'Very well. We'll leave it at that. But just don't let it go any further. You sometimes behave in a very eccentric way, Brenda. Your relationships can be very shallow.'

'Oh no. I'm a very conventional person, I'm afraid. I'm not brave, like you.'

They took their cups of coffee and sat by the gas fire – Brenda pulling her short skirt down to hide her stocking tops from her admirer as best she could – and Susan took up the story.


Alan was late at the office on the second day of the diet. Susan was watering the pot plants with a green and red watering-can from Heals, especially designed for watering pot plants. Alan was bad-tempered. His agent had appreciated his novel, but his life had not thereby been transformed, and he felt cheated.

'Oh, Mr Sussman!' said Susan, reproachfully. 'You're late.'

'Well?'

'You're late.'

'I am not late. I am just not as early as usual. If you can't be polite at least try to be accurate.'

'I suppose your being so often late is a protest against your coming to the office at all. I think it would be sensible for you to hand in your notice altogether. Why spend your days doing something you don't like? You only live once.'

'It is too early in the morning for this sort of conversation. I might as well be at home.' He hung his coat behind the provided curtain, and looked discreetly down at his stomach. It seemed much the same.

'It is not early for me. I've been up since five.'

'Whatever for?'

'The light is good at that time for painting. The whole world seems different, somehow, when everyone else is asleep. It's unobserved, and it shows.'

'You must show me some of your work, sometime.'

'I am very particular to whom I show my paintings.'

'You must try and be a little more particular about your typing,' was all he said, looking at the list of the day's engagements which she had typed.

She was wearing a white ribbed jersey, which seemed too small for her, an abbreviated skirt, and a leather belt which hung around her hips. He thought it scarcely seemed suitable attire for a secretary in an advertising agency. It would never have been allowed in a permanent girl.

'How can it be,' he said, 'that I have no meetings until late this afternoon?'

She sat down behind her typewriter and spoke coldly, for she had been snubbed.

'Today was the day you were supposed to be going to the Sussex shampoo factory. They waited as long as they could, and I rang Mrs Sussman and she said you'd only just left, so Mr Venery went in your place. That's why.'

'Oh.'

'They thought Mr Venery would do just as well.'

'Oh. Did they.'

'And I dare say they were right. He can be very impressive when he talks.'

'You are becoming quite impossible. I know you like to make it clear that you are not by nature a secretary. But since you are being paid, couldn't you at least act the role? It is very disconcerting to have a girl like you sitting about all day.'

'Thank you.' She smiled.

'I didn't mean that as a compliment, either. Offices are serious places, where work must always take precedence over everything else. I dare say to a girl as emancipated and free-thinking as you, the work we actually do must appear strange, even bizarre. I can see that to an outsider the vision of a group of grey-suited gentlemen of high moral principle and even higher income sitting round a table discussing the attitude of teenage girls to dandruff must seem somewhat ludicrous. But teenage girls have dandruff. And they need and like to have it cured. And a great many people work in factories making the cure, and others like us work at selling it in its most acceptable and cheapest form. It has its own kind of dignity, the work we do – if only because it is so open to mockery. It is easy enough to laugh at dandruff – just so long as you haven't got it.'

'You could use that as a headline. I wasn't laughing at dandruff in particular, as it happens, or at you. You've sold out, that's all, and I think it's sad. It's a waste of your potentiality. I'm sure if someone had said to you when you were fifteen that you'd end up selling dandruff cures you'd have committed suicide on the spot, and perhaps you would have been right to do so. People have a duty to their talents.'

'I have not "ended up", as you put it. And I sell a great many other things besides shampoo. And I think, incidentally, you are too old to be wearing that gear. It's for teenagers, not grown women.'

'Why do you feel the need to attack me? Why do you want to hurt my feelings all the time? Do my knees worry you so much?'

'No. It is not so much your knees, as you well know, but your thighs.'

'I am sorry,' she said. 'If it worries you I will wear skirts to my ankles. If you ask me to do anything, I will.'

'Good heavens,' he said, 'good heavens it's much too early for this kind of thing.'

'I told you it didn't seem early to me. I've been up for hours.'

He circled her.

'What am I going to do for the rest of the day, with nothing arranged? And you quite wilfully tormenting me?'

'Act like the middle-aged company man you delude yourself you are. Spend a useful day stabilising your relations with the rest of the staff. Write memos to remind your superiors that you exist – it seems to be necessary. Go on a tour of inspection, there must be something to inspect. Ask your staff if they're happy.'

'Are you?'

'I'm always happy.'

'I don't believe you.'

'I always do what I want.'

'You are very fortunate, then.'

'Not fortunate. Sensible. I dreamt about you last night.'

'What?'

'It was very private. It was marvellous.'

'Good heavens,' he said, 'good heavens. What do you see in me? I'm a middle-aged man with a middle-aged mind. You are young, beautiful, talented, intelligent and truly, truly, remarkable.'

'You have a wonderful turn of phrase, just sometimes: did you know that? But a lot of the time you speak platitudes. What

61

element in yourself is it that you hide from? You use clichés as a shelter, and it is not necessary. I hope you don't use them when you write.'

'It is a lovely day. Shall we go for a walk in the park? How very irregular! But we could talk about books. Did you know I have just written a novel?'

'Yes, as a matter of fact.'

'Would you be interested in reading it?'

'Oh yes.'

'I haven't got a copy at the office. There are two at home, though. I'll bring one in. It might interest you. Many people might be shocked – but not, I think you.'

They put on the red 'engaged' light above his office door and went out, by different staircases, into the street and met in the park. He felt the same pleasure as when he had played truant as a child; she felt agreeably conspiratorial. The sun shone.

'What did you have for breakfast?' she asked.

'Eggs.'

'I don't think food is at all important, but I can see that for people who are used to it, going without would be most difficult. I don't think you ought to, actually. You are a shadowy enough figure as it is.'

'Shadowy?'

'You lack substance. Men do tend to lack substance in women's eyes. They are figments of lust, vague sources of despair. I think the least a man can do, in the circumstances, is to endeavour to exist well and truly in the flesh. I believe in you on account of your being so solid. It is the other way round with women. A woman has all too much substance in a man's eyes at the best of times. That is why men like women to be slim. Her lack of flesh negates her. The less of her there is, the less notice he need take of her. The more like a male she appears to be, the safer he feels.'

'My wife doesn't half fight back then.'

'Is she *very* fat?'

But he was silent.

'Did you used to be a painter?' she asked presently, returning to safer ground.

'Why do you ask?'

'From the way you pick up a pencil. From the way you scribble over bad layouts. You seem to know exactly what you're doing.'

'You are very quick. I did study once.'

'What happened?'

'I had a couple of shows. But it was hungry work. Then I married. You have to earn a living. Once you embark on family life it is too late to do anything else. Thoughts of self-expression fly out the window.'

'Not if you have courage. I think perhaps you lack courage.'

'If true courage lies in doing what you don't want to do, from a sense of duty, then I am a truly courageous man.'

'Not at all. True courage lies in doing what you want to do, and not caring whom you hurt.'

'True courage,' he said, 'lies in employing temporary secretaries with beautiful legs and wayward thoughts.'

He kissed her in the bushes where he was sure no one from the office could possibly see. She was vastly pleased, and took the afternoon off – he could scarcely refuse – and went home and told William all about it.

And all the way home in his taxi that evening he brooded about Esther's malice in plotting to cook his omelette in butter the night before.


'It all sounds rather sordid to me,' said Brenda, sipping her coffee, 'secretary and boss and stolen idylls in the park. It's like the *News of the World*. My mother always said that men in offices were underemployed. That's why she would prefer me to marry a professional man. They are so worn out by work they don't cause trouble. She is very funny, my mother, in a sinister suburban way.'

'It was only a kiss,' said Susan, 'but afterwards all the colours in the park seemed stronger and the trees made strange shapes in the sky and when I went home and told William, I found my knees were trembling and so I knew I meant what I was saying. I was in love. The same man, not my boss, would probably have made no impression on me at all, I am honest enough to admit it. Status is a great aphrodisiac. His name was in black type on the telephone list and if you work for an organisation like Zo's, even temporarily, these things have the power to affect you.'

'What do you mean, told William?'

'I explained to him about Alan, and how it would be better for him to move out because it wouldn't be fair to him, me being in love with someone else. He quite understood. We have a very civilised relationship. He went home. It all seemed, at the time, to fit in very well.'

'You were presuming, weren't you? I mean that more would happen between you and Alan than just a kiss in the park? You were getting rid of William before you were sure of Alan. I mean next time you met him he might have pretended it never happened. I've met men like that before.'

The foreign gentleman held out his cup. Brenda filled it.

'His bladder will burst,' said Susan. 'How can any man drink so much coffee?'

'It's because he doesn't want to leave. The coffee is his excuse for staying. He is suffering greatly on our account.'

'Your account.'

'It is true,' said Brenda, 'that his eyes follow me, not you. I wonder why.'

'Perhaps in the country he comes from they like their women to have massive legs.'

'What country do you think it is?'

'The Lebanon?'

'Where's that?'

'I haven't the faintest idea.'

'Perhaps Ceylon or somewhere like that. He seems an educated man to me.'

'Now how do you deduce that?'

'He has a very intelligent expression in his eyes. Don't you think he's very attractive? I like a silent man.'

'I don't. I like words. Alan handled words beautifully.'

'Susan, if William is so civilised and understanding, why isn't he here now?'

'Because his wife's having a baby. I don't see why you're complaining. You're only here in the flat because he's not.'

'I'm sorry, I'm sure.'

'I didn't mean it like that. But naturally a girl prefers to live with a man.'

'What about all those Kensington secretaries, sharing flats with one another?'

'Cowards, or lesbians,' said Susan.

'Surely!' Brenda was disbelieving.

The foreign man closed his eyes. Brenda moved over and gently stroked his forehead, even as she protested.

'Brenda!' Susan was scandalised. 'You hardly know him!'

But Brenda stroked on. Susan rose and went back to the pub, leaving them together.


'By the fourth day of the diet I was in despair,' said Esther to Phyllis. 'I can't really bear to think about it. Shall we go and have some curry? It would do me good. I have hardly been out of this place for days.'

'You'll have to change,' said Phyllis. 'You can't go out like that.'

'Why not?'

'You're covered with soup.'

'If I don't care, why should you? I didn't bring anything with me when I left. I don't need clothes. I don't want anyone to look at me; it's their misfortune if they do. Are you ashamed to be seen out with me?'

'No.'

'You're lying. People have been ashamed to be seen out with me as long as I can remember. I was a very dirty little girl. My mother used to tell me so. She's a very small neat woman, as you know, and I by comparison, overflowed. I seemed to have more surfaces than she, and every single one of them picked up dirt. While I was married to Alan I tried very hard to be clean. I dusted and swept and polished myself as well as the house. I bathed every day, changed my clothes twice a day, bought new ones perpetually; had everything dry-cleaned. It is a very expensive business, being clean. I sewed on buttons, too. None of it was my true nature. In trying to be clean I contorted myself. This is what I am really like: I shall pretend no longer. If you are too ashamed to go into an Indian restaurant with me as I am, it doesn't matter to me in the least. I don't really want to go out anyway. I have lots of English curry in the cupboard.'

'You can't still be hungry.'

'It has nothing to do with hunger for God's sake.'

'It's psychological, you mean.'

Esther did not deign to reply. She picked out a tin of curry and a tin of savoury rice from the shelf.

'It's not real curry, this, of course. Real curry is very tricky to make. You use spices, added at precise intervals, and coconut milk. It's not just a matter of making a stew and adding curry powder and raisins and bananas. You have to devote a whole day to making a true curry. It is all a great waste of time and energy, but it keeps women occupied, and that's important. If they had a spare hour or two they might look at their husbands and laugh, mightn't they? I am glad you stopped me going out. If I leave this place goodness knows where my footsteps might not take me.'

'I didn't stop you going out. You stopped yourself.'

'Did I? How fortunate. Now where were we? One of the strange things about not eating is how clearly you begin to see things. By the end of a week I could see myself very clearly indeed, and it was not comfortable. My home was not comfortable either. It seemed a cold and chilly place, and I could see no point in the objects that filled it, that had to be eternally dusted and polished and cared for. Why? They were not human. They had no importance other than their appearance. They were bargains, that was their only merit. I had bought them cheap, yet I had more than enough money to spend, so where was the achievement? Those old things, picked up and rescued and put down on a shelf to be appreciated, were taking over my whole life. They were quaint, oh yes, and some were even pretty, but they were no justification for my being alive. Running a house is not a sensible occupation for a grown woman. Dusting and sweeping, cooking and washing up — it is work for the sake of work, an eternal circle which lasts from the day you get married until the day you die, or are put into an old folks' home because you are too feeble to pick up some man's dirty clothes and wash them any more. For whose sake did I do it? Not my own, certainly. Not Peter's — he could as well have lived in a tree as in a house for all the notice he took of his surroundings. Not Alan's. Alan only searched for flaws: if he could not find dirt with which to chide me, if he could not find waste with which to rebuke me, then he was disappointed. And daily I tried to disappoint him. To spend my life waging war against Alan, which was what my housewifeliness amounted to, endeavouring to prove a female competence which was the last thing he wanted or needed to know about — what a waste of time this was! Was I to die still polishing and dusting, washing and ironing; seeking to find in this my fulfilment? Imprisoning Alan as well as myself in this structure of bricks and mortar we called our home? We would have been as happy, or as miserable, in a cave. We would have been freer and more ourselves, let's admit it, in *two* caves.'

'Caves are nasty damp places. You would have TB in no time. And I don't see Alan as a caveman. Now Gerry, I could see Gerry in a cave.'

'Oh, you are an inveterate little woman, aren't you? You love having a bully for a husband.'

'Gerry's not a bully. He is very strong-willed and not very good at controlling his emotions, and he speaks his mind, and he is very highly-sexed, but he's not a bully. And he needs me. And I like having the house nice when he comes home, and the smell of food cooking to welcome him and everything looking neat and tidy.'

'I bet you put on lipstick for the great home-coming, too. And a fresh dress and comb your hair, and put on a welcome-home-darling smile, just like in the women's magazines. God, what an almighty bore.'

'That's silly. He looks forward all day to coming home.'

'That's what he says, you make him say it; but what does he feel? What does he think? What do any of them think? When I looked at Alan during that week I saw a stranger, and a hostile stranger at that. Someone who conned me and betrayed me and laughed at me behind my back. All these years of marriage, I could see, he had been laughing at me, playing with me, using me and my money, and caring nothing for me at all. When he smiled at me it was to hide the sneer of derision on his lips; when he touched me and embraced me it was the worst insult of all, because he had to steel himself to do it. I knew he did. Because he touched me to keep me quiet. He lusted after someone half my age, and half my size.'

'Those are terrible feelings to have about anyone, let alone a husband. And Alan's not like that. Alan's not a sly kind of person.'

'I'm not saying he is. I'm just saying that's what it felt like to me, that particular week. Juliet did what she could to make matters worse, too.'

On the seventh day of the diet Juliet sat at the living-room table polishing the silver with impudent inefficiency, and singing. Esther, in the adjoining kitchen, clattered pots and pans to indicate disapproval of her cleaner's merriment. The more she banged and crashed the sweeter Juliet sang. Then Esther appeared in the doorway, staring full at her, but Juliet sang on, and refrained from speeding up the rate of her polishing, or even of pressing harder upon the metal.

'Juliet, if you rubbed a little harder it would come up better.'

'Bad for the surface, Mrs Sussman, rubbing too hard. Gently does it, with the good stuff.'

'You just *say* that, Juliet. It's not true.'

Juliet put her cloth down. 'Are you saying I don't know how to polish silver?'

'Yes,' said Esther with desperation.

'Then perhaps you should find someone else to do it. To speak frankly, since you and Mr Sussman started not eating, this house has not been a pleasure to come into.'

'I would rather you didn't leave, Juliet.'

'You are quite right not to want me to go. You wouldn't get anyone else to work in a place like this. Things everywhere. Nothing new. Everything old-fashioned and dingy.'

'It's very fashionable, as it happens.'

'And the atmosphere! You wouldn't get anyone else to work in this kind of atmosphere.'

Esther was terrified. 'What do you mean?'

'Well,' said Juliet, in a more kindly fashion, 'I dare say it does take all sorts, and to be frank, your home is nothing to some I've seen.'

'You'll stay, you mean? Please do. Don't be upset.'

'I'll see you through a bit longer, because obviously you are not yourself. I think it is very foolish of you to ruin your health and your temper in this way, if you don't mind my saying so. Some of us are made fat and some of us are made thin, and that's all there is to it. You'll lose your husband if you carry on like this. He can't much fancy this glimpse of the Real You.'

'But it's he who makes me do it.'

'Not satisfied with what he's got? Is that it? That's husbands all over. Ungrateful pigs. You do everything for them, you bring up their kids, you cook their food, you wash their clothes, you warm their beds, you fuss over your face day after day so they'll fancy you, you wear yourself out to keep them happy and at the end of it all, what happens? They find someone else they fancy more. Someone young some man hasn't had the chance to wear out yet. Marriage is a con trick. A girl should marry a rich man, then at least she'd have a fur coat to keep her warm in her old age.'

'I don't know who you're talking about, Juliet, but it's certainly not *my* husband. If you do want to go on working for me, and I pay you 8/- an hour, which is 3/- above market rates, I suggest you get on with it.'

'Oh go on, Mrs Sussman, just as we were getting on so nicely.

Have a nice hot piece of toast with jam on it. And some nice milky coffee.'

'No, that would be cheating. Alan will kill me if I cheat.'

'You don't think he's cheating away at his office, wherever he is? What do you think he does when you're not looking?'

'Just get on with the polishing, Juliet.'

Juliet started singing. Esther went back to the kitchen, and tiny tears ran down her wide cheeks.


When Susan went back to her flat she found Brenda pacing the room in a dressing-gown. She seemed surprised: her large grey eyes were opened very wide. The man from overseas lay, fully clothed even to his carefully knotted tie, asleep on the hearth-rug.

'What an extraordinary thing,' said Brenda. 'How strange life is. They are right, love knows no boundaries of creed or colour. It strikes out of a clear sky. I am glad I left home. Things like this only happen in London.'

'I should be careful if I were you. Perhaps he has a strange disease.'

'Oh no, he's not like that at all. He is a very gentle, sensitive, discreet kind of person.'

'How do you know? He doesn't speak.'

'You can tell,' she said. 'You can tell from the way he breathes.'

'I think your behaviour is quite extraordinary. It might almost be called promiscuous. Please ask him to leave at once.'

'He's asleep. We'll have to wait until he wakes up, or it will be bad for his health. It is most unjust of you to call me names. You are always advocating free spontaneous behaviour, yet the slightest sign of life from me and you try to make me feel I have behaved badly. But I haven't, I really haven't. I have done nothing at all to be ashamed of. Everything I did, I did from love. It flowed out of me. It was a wonderful feeling, like being part of the earth.'

'What did happen exactly? I mean physically, not spiritually.'

'I can't remember, I really can't remember. Susan, have we any drink?'

She wandered out of the pool of light in the centre of the room into the darker perimeter, where Susan's paints and jars and brushes and clothing made black patches on the black floor.

'I feel awful all of a sudden,' she said, 'really I do. It is all your fault. I felt lovely until you came home. Free and happy and beautiful and taken by surprise. Now it's all nasty.'

'I am not your mother and you are not a little girl. I do think, however, that this kind of behaviour is not in your nature. It doesn't become you. You should go back home and marry a nice bank-clerk, and only fornicate, if absolutely necessary, with someone harmless like the milkman.'

'Supposing I'm pregnant?'

'Then you would be very foolish. Do you have his name and address?'

'No.'

'Then get it.'

'When he wakes. Will you go on telling me about Alan, and we can pretend he's not there?'

'You can't shut your eyes to realities. There is turps in that bottle, not wine.'

'Perhaps I should drink it. Perhaps death is what I deserve.'

'Death is a major and beautiful thing. What you have done was merely trivial and sordid. You should not speak about the two in the same sentence. Put the bottle down. You don't even deserve to die.'

'Don't talk to me like that. At least I don't go around trying to break up marriages.'

'I don't try to break up marriages. If marriages break up because of me that is scarcely my fault – it is the wife's fault for being my inferior. It may not appear fair on the surface, but it was what Christ was talking about when he said to them that hath shall be given, and from them that hath not shall be taken away.'

'But that's awful. I'm sure men value other things in their

76

wives. I read in the paper about how Germans rate thrift in a wife as the most important thing, and then cleanliness, and then fidelity, and good looks came way down at the bottom of the list and intelligence last of all.'

'Do you want to marry a German?'

'No.'

'Well then.'

'But I don't want to get married and have my husband go off. I think it's wrong for girls to go with married men.'

'What about him?' The man on the hearth-rug stirred.

'I don't know if he's married. He hasn't said he's married.'

'I expect his wife is crying at home this very minute with the children sobbing at her knee. I expect that's why he hasn't bothered to learn English, in case anyone rebukes him with his wife and makes him feel bad.'

'Don't say such things. He's a gay young student, carefree and vital.'

'You reckon?'

'I just don't know. To tell you the truth, I don't know much more about him now than I did before. I wish he'd get up and go away and then I wouldn't have to worry.'

'Perhaps you take a very masculine attitude to sex. Perhaps

that's what's wrong. The loving-and-leaving syndrome is not natural in a girl.'

'Alan was old enough to be your father. Perhaps you have a daughter-father syndrome.'

'Exactly, I don't deny it. He was so grey and middle-aged and clever and superior and in control, and his flies were so tightly buttoned, and the excitement of dissolving him and stripping away the veneer and turning him into a naked little boy again – and not even knowing whether I could do it – it was wonderfully exhilarating. And to be so frighteningly dependent, all of a sudden, quite against one's better judgement, upon someone else's good opinion; to want to impress; to want to attract; to want above all just to be noticed; to feel so nervous and insecure; to worry in case one's breath stank; these were all symptoms I had never known before. These were the symptoms of unrequited love, and they were both horrible and glorious. I felt truly alive at last. I don't recommend it, Brenda, for you. You are not tough enough to withstand pain; that is why you make sure your relationships are always so shallow. Well, yours is one way of living. But I prefer myself to enter wholeheartedly into whatever it is I'm doing, even if it entails suffering. That is some of William's home-made elderberry wine you are sniffing. It is not supposed to be drunk for another six months, but I think we could open a jar, and drink to him and his baby, and to Alan. And don't say I am breaking up William's marriage either, because I'm not, or he wouldn't be back with his wife now, would he, and you wouldn't be using my flat as a knocking shop, and none of any of this upsetting business would have happened. We would all be as happy as once we were.'

On the eighth day of the diet Alan sang, sitting in his chair in his empty office with his feet on the desk. He was happy. There was an almost empty bottle of champagne at his elbow. Susan came into his office after lunch. She had been transferred, at Alan's request, to the research department. It put her at a disadvantage.

'Why are you singing?'

'Because I'm happy.'

'You've been drinking.'

'I have been drinking but I do not have to drink in order to be happy. Just occasionally I am happy, and then nothing can stop me, neither flesh nor fowl nor drink nor wife nor even you, my dear.'

'Why should you think I want to stop you being happy? I want you to be happy.'

'Oh no. *You* want to be happy.'

'What are we going to do, Alan?'

'Do?' Alan took his feet off the desk abruptly, dropped the champagne bottle into the wastepaper basket, and straightened his tie. 'Do? About what?'

'About us. Sometimes you make me feel like some vulgar office girl. I think you do it on purpose.'

'But you know you are not, don't you. You are a very fine and

79

sensitive person, with great talent and worthy of better than me. Yes?'

'You are mocking me.'

'You have no sense of humour. That is your whole problem. It is quite remarkable.'

'And you are incapable of being serious about anything. That's much worse.'

'I am sorry. Am I being very disagreeable?'

'Yes.'

'I am hungry. I haven't really had much to drink. It is just that it's gone straight to my head, because my stomach is empty.'

'I don't know any longer what sort of person you want me to be.'

'I don't know what I want. I don't know anything except that I was happy before you came in, thinking about you. It is odd that when the reality of you appears all happiness should evaporate, to be replaced by feelings so resentful and defensive that I am now quite agitated. You are looking marvellous.'

'Are you coming round this evening? I need to know, so I can buy food.'

'I don't come to visit you to eat, do I? Remember I am a married man, and on a diet.'

'I wish you would eat more. You are nicer when you've eaten.'

'Come and sit on my knee.'

'I'm too heavy, and someone might come in.'

'True. Also, it is a vulgar habit between boss and secretary.'

'I just don't know what you think or feel about me. You talk as if you hated me and you act as if you loved me.'

'Be careful.'

'What of?'

'That word. It leads to more trouble than any other single word in the English language. Shouldn't you be working?'

'Tony White never comes back until half past three. He's always drunk. He smells. He leans over me and breathes into my ear. It's horrible.'

'Poor Susan.'

'Since you are being so disagreeable and strange I'm going back to my office. If you don't mind Tony White putting his hand up my skirt, why should I?'

'He's a dirty old man then, isn't he?'

'He's no older than you.'

'That's quite different. Oh Susan, I am a hungry man. The champagne has filled me with bubbles but bubbles are not food. Food is the supremest of pleasures.'

'Spoken to a mistress, that is not a compliment.'

'I am out of my mind. Am I thinner, Susan? Do I begin to lack the substance you want me to have? I dream all night, as I haven't dreamt since I was twenty. I dream of strange and marvellous things. I dream of fish and chips and bread and butter and cups of sweet tea. I dream of ship-loads of boiling jam cleaving their way through the polar ice-caps. I dream of – oh Susan, I have such dreams as life itself is made of.'

'You're laughing at me again.'

'Why not? I am allowed to have poetic fancies as well as you. I take you very seriously. When you sit and wave your legs at me they are the most beautiful legs I have ever seen. You make me young again. There is a gap between stocking top and knicker which excites me beyond belief. I want to eat it. I shall visit you this evening.'

'You are crude. You are only interested in my body.'

'And when you first waved your stocking tops at me, you did so more crudely than any other secretary I have ever had, and that is saying something. You had your way with me. But I must remind you that I am an old man. You are a child and you are playing with dangerous things. When children take their games seriously, it ends in tears. With grown-ups, it ends in suicides, divorce, and delinquent children. Be careful what you do.'

'There is only twenty years between us. You are not old at all, just experienced.'

'Compared to you, I may say, I suspect that I am indeed young in experience. Yet I have my aims, my fancies. And I am older than you, much older, in years. Youth to me is a magic thing, although to you it may seem a burden. For I am a balding plump old man, and I don't want to be. I dream that you might rescue me, and infect me with youth and hope again and all the things I have lost through the years, along with ties and pocket handkerchiefs. But age wins in the end. It must. Age turns even lust to ashes. I am an honest man, and even though it goes against my interests, I warn you here and now that in a week or so I shall have a fit of coughing and take to my own warm familiar bed and forget all about yours. Yet perhaps I delude myself that this might hurt you? I know so little about your generation. All I can tell you is that my intentions towards you are entirely dishonourable. If you are likely to take me seriously, stop now. Stop waving your legs at me. I am not strong enough to withstand you. This diet weakens me. You are taking monstrous advantage of a poor weak hungry man. I never thought to be an adulterer.'

'You credit me with no feelings at all. You see me as some kind of sexual vulture preying upon your flesh. You are very old-fashioned. You think that if a woman takes any kind of initiative she is cheap and worthless. In fact I have given up a great deal on your account, because I have faith in my own feelings and I am prepared to suffer for them — even your rejection of everything about me that isn't just my body. I offer you a great deal and you turn your back on it.'

'I hadn't noticed myself doing any such thing.'

'Please try and understand me.'

'Very well. What have you offered me?'

'My difference. Whatever it is that makes me different from every other woman in the world. You scorn it. You see me not as a person, just as a woman. I want to be a person.'

'Girls given to adulterous affairs must learn not to expect too much.'

'You try and hurt me in order to spare yourself. I have great faith in you, all the same. I think you are capable of more than sitting behind an office desk thinking about dandruff, and practising your silly defences on me. I am trying to rescue you. I am offering you a chance of escaping into a better richer honester life. It will hurt, but it will be better than what you have now, which is nothing, nothing, except boredom and dullness and sterility for the rest of your life.'

'I don't feel at all happy any more,' he said. 'I hope you are satisfied.'

She put her arms around his neck and snuffled his ear and told him everything was all right.

'When you stop talking,' he said, 'you are wonderful. You are a comforting delicious child, all peaches and cream. Your breasts are like melons, your breath is like honey, your hair is like — no, spun-silk is inedible.'

'Spun toffee?'

'Wonderful! I would rather make love to you than eat a dozen cream cakes, and that is the most sincere compliment you are ever likely to receive in your whole life. Now go and type for Tony White and tell him to keep his hands to himself, and kick him in the balls if he won't. Or threaten him with a memo in triplicate, which would hurt him even more.'

Susan was either crying or her eyes were watering with indignation. Brenda, who had never seen Susan cry, chose to think that it was the latter emotion. Susan put on a Sidney Bechet record and danced around the prostrate man on the floor. It was a solitary, lonely, despairing dance, sexual but entirely self-preoccupied, prompted by his existence but on the whole disparaging of it. Her body seemed composed of two disparate parts. Her top half swayed like a weak tree in a strong gale: her buttocks pumped up and down mechanically, like pistons. Brenda felt embarrassed by this exhibition of passion, and was glad when whatever madness it was left Susan, and she sat down, peacefully, and sipped elderberry wine.

'Love will always cause pain,' Susan observed, 'because the passion is so much nobler and greater than its objects. Men stand as trivial, flawed, puny things before the majesty of love. Love possesses one, but there is nothing fit for it to be released upon. So it is a perpetual agony.'

'Perhaps you should be a nun. Then you could be a bride of Christ, and then perhaps you would be satisfied.'

'I begin to understand nuns,' said Susan. 'I never thought I would. I suppose I can thank Alan for that. But I believe one has to be a virgin. And it would never do for me, anyway. I need men to define me: to give me an idea of what I am. If I didn't have boyfriends I don't think I would exist. I would fly apart in all directions. So I must live my life in perpetual pain, if I want to live at all.'

'I feel quite happy quite a lot of the time,' said Brenda, as one who apologises.

'Oh you! You are just a whore at heart. I was quite wrong about you and being a mother. Your thighs are money-makers, not creators.'

'It is a funny kind of love you talk about,' said Brenda, incensed. 'It seems to have nothing to do with the man loved. You have too much of it inside. It overflows and attaches itself at random, like a kind of blood-sucking slug. If I was a man I would most certainly want to brush it off.'

Susan looked at the painting on her easel. 'My painting makes me sick too. It just makes matters worse. There is no point in it. It's just more of me, spreading into another dimension. If you're a woman you never win. Look at it. It's so bloody fucking personal. I don't know why I bother.'

'Why are you sitting here listening to me?' asked Esther of Phyllis. 'Why aren't you at home warming Gerry's slippers, or sulking, or putting on a flimsy nightie to tempt him, or whatever you are accustomed to doing at this time of night?'

'He had to work late at the office, so I thought I wouldn't be there when he came home, just to show him.'

'Show him what?'

'That I can have a life of my own, too.'

'Do you play this game all the time, Phyllis, or only some of the time?'

'Game? It isn't a game. It's very serious, and very painful.'

'Supposing he comes home and finds you gone and goes straight out to revenge himself?'

'I know. It does happen, I suppose. It is very worrying. Perhaps I should go home.'

'I suggest you do.'

'You haven't told me a thing yet. You've just talked and talked. No, I don't think I should go home. Gerry must be taught a lesson.'

'No wonder he looks elsewhere.'

'It's not that Gerry *looks*. It's that unscrupulous women place themselves where he can't help seeing them. Some women are like that. And if he's angry with me – Gerry gets angry very easily – then terrible things happen.'

'Terrible for whom?'

'For me. And for Gerry. It complicates his life, and he has a strong sense of duty. He wouldn't keep seeing his wife otherwise.'

'You're his wife, Phyllis.'

'His ex-wife, I mean. It's hard to remember. I feel she's his real wife, you see, and I'm in the wrong to be living with him at all. Please go on with your story. Can I have some of that luncheon meat, please?'

Esther cut Phyllis a slab of luncheon meat, and another one for herself. They gnawed its pink flabbiness with pleasure.

'Talking of girls standing in the way to be looked at,' said Esther, 'it was exactly what this stupid child Susan Pierce was doing. Alan was not exactly a romantic figure, but he had written a book and that was enough to set her going. Her usual style, I gather, is any man of letters, preferably married, who has an assured future and frequent mentions in the Sunday papers. A very suburban creature, I thought her, and her true stereo-typed self very easily got the upper hand. The slightest stirring in her loins – and Alan is remarkably good at the promise of pleasure, if not its fulfilment – and her suburban little heart cried love. And that was not what Alan meant at all.'

'What did he want, then?'

'He was hungry. A hungry man grabs what he can get.'

'But you were hungry too.'

'Hunger made him aggressive. It merely bored me. So much

88

of my daily life had been taken up by shopping and cooking, and eating and washing-up after the cooking, and now it had all evaporated. There was nothing left to do in the long hungry hours but work myself up into a state about Alan's betrayal of me.'

'How did you know he had betrayed you? How could you tell?'

'The upheaval in my routine had left me paranoic, I admit. I would have suspected him of infidelity with his secretary, simply because she was temporary and named Susan, whether I had grounds for my suspicion or not. I had no grounds, but I suspected, and as it transpired, quite fortuitously, I was right.'

'I don't regard Gerry's affairs as a threat to my marriage. They are very trivial. He says so and I agree.'

'What other choice have you but to agree? Divorce? You are not brave enough to be a single woman. You are a coward. You have played at being helpless for so long that now you are. And Gerry knows it. He doesn't have to bother. Your friends are Gerry's friends, not yours at all. Your home is Gerry's home, bought with Gerry's money. You just don't exist without him. And again, a single woman over thirty is an object of pity, or so you think. So you agree with Gerry that such masculine affairs are trivial; you tell yourself it is not in a man's nature to be monogamous; but neither of these things are any more true of men than they are of women, and your misery is no one's fault but your own because you are craven and a betrayer of your sex. You suck up to the enemy. I despise you.'

'Thank you very much, I'm sure. I love Gerry, as it so happens.'

'You are incurable. You comfort yourself with words. I will continue. I was getting thinner. I had lost eight lbs. in just over a week. I was pleased with myself, but no one would allow me comfort. I was tormented.'

On the ninth day of the diet Peter said to his mother, as he sat at the kitchen table eating steak pie and chips from the fish-and-chip shop round the corner, 'I think you are out of your mind.' His mother was eating three ounces of cottage cheese and two tablespoonfuls of spinach. Alan was not yet back from the office. 'Why don't you eat? No one cares whether you are fat or thin. Let's face it, you are out of the age group where it matters. You just be a nice cosy comfy mum and leave it at that! What more do you want? You've got a nice home and a good husband and I'm no trouble to you, and an easy life – and when you think of the lives most women have to lead – seven children and a drunken husband – I think there's something rather awful about middle-aged middle-class people going on diets, when all over the world people are starving to death – literally –'

'My troubles are not outside me,' said Esther, 'they are inside me. Those are the worst troubles of all.'

That evening Alan and Esther lay in the double bed they had owned for eighteen years. It was five foot wide. Once they had occupied, happily, the two feet in the centre. Now they used the peripheries.

They lay staring up at the ceiling, hungry, and presently they began to talk, which was not their usual custom in bed.

'Steak and kidney pudding,' said Esther, 'with mushrooms and oysters and the gravy oozing out. And mashed potatoes and a cauliflower cheese, all golden and bubbling on top, with bits of green stalk right down at the bottom where the sauce is thinner and buttery.'

'Hare soup,' replied Alan, 'with fresh rolls and lots of butter. And then roast duck with roast potatoes and green peas. Followed by apple pie and cheese and biscuits. A Brie, I think, just at the right point of squishiness, with that slight and marvellous taste of something on the verge of going bad. Something you can suspect of being rotten, but you know you're allowed to eat.'

'I'd have apple pie. You break through the crust and it's juicy underneath. Chocolate mousse is nice of course, with chopped walnuts on top. With whipped cream flavoured with rum.'

'Or apricot crumble. My mother used to make that.'

'I know.'

'That's why I never get it, I suppose.'

'Don't be silly. We all know, of course, what a marvellous cook your mother was and how beautifully she kept her house. How the clean warm wind blew freshly through the windows, which were always opened in every bedroom at the same time every morning. That it was an Indian wind, of course, you

91

forget. That there is nothing outside our windows but a fall of damp black soot from a sulphurous heaven you prefer to overlook. You still make faces at the closed bedroom windows. Men are very good at making faces over domestic details. They say nothing, but with the merest look they can drain all joy from any minimal sense of domestic achievement one may have painfully acquired.'

'You speak out of intimate knowledge of the domestic nature of dozens of men, I notice. You must have crammed a great deal into your life before you met me. And indeed, I may say, after.'

'I did. Another thing you forget is that your mother had some twelve Indian slaves whereas I have the dubious advantage of a daily help a couple of hours every day.'

'I was making no comparison between my mother and you. It was you who decided I had. All I said was that my mother made apricot crumble, and I liked it, and for some reason I never get it from you.'

'You could always cook it yourself.'

'Charming! Back from a hard day at the office to cook my own dinner. Why don't you ask me to sweep the floors too?'

'The more you complain about your hard day at the office, the less plausible it seems. Just sitting at a desk all day, talking, writing, lifting up the telephone, do you call that work?'

'People who have never worked in offices have no idea of the tensions, the decisions and the crises which attend one's every hour. I am worn out by midday, exhausted by the time I get home.'

'So I'd noticed.'

'What is that supposed to mean?'

'Oh never mind. I'm too fat and unattractive anyway. Unlike your – what's her name – Audrey? Janet? Susan? That's it. Susan. The willowy, artistic one.'

'For God's sake what do you want? We've been married nearly twenty years.'

'Oh don't pretend –'

'What is the matter with you?'

'I think she should leave. It's not fair to me.'

'Now what in the world –? What earthly reason have you –'

'You only talk about her when you're drunk, that's why. Not a mention of her when you're sober. You inhibit your conversation on her account. The only way I ever know anything about you is by listening to you when you're drunk, did you know that?'

'You speak as if I was some kind of alcoholic.'

'Perhaps you are. Anyway, there it is. You don't talk about Susan when you're sober.'

'I thought I was supposed never to be sober.'

'Don't be silly.'

'The truth is, of course, that I daren't talk about her. You are so impossibly jealous. You are mad. It is this diet. I think you had better give it up. I can't live with you while you're like this.'

'But you will carry on, of course, being so strong-willed and self-disciplined.'

'Yes.'

'Charming.' Esther sat upright in bed. The tops of her arms were flabby, but her flesh was still very white and smooth. 'So I've got to be fat and ugly while you get thin and carry on with your secretary.'

'You are quite impossible. It's no use trying to reason with you at all.'

Tears fell out of Esther's eyes.

'It's not fair to me. It's not fair. It's not my fault I'm fat.'

'Well it's certainly not mine. If it's not one thing it's another. Go to sleep. Stop behaving like a little girl. You'll feel better in the morning. Incidentally —'

'Yes —' said Esther, comforted by this exercise in luxurious authority, and wanting to hear more.

94

'Marriage isn't a prison. You remember what Gerry was saying the other evening? Unfaithful husbands are made by jealous wives.'

They lay silent for some minutes, both with their eyes open, carefully not touching, despite the dip in the middle of their marital mattress. Presently Esther stretched out her hand to lay it on his belly.

'Alan?'

'Go to sleep.'

'I'm sorry.'

'You always are, afterwards. Why do you start?'

'I don't know. I thought it was you who started. Anyway it doesn't matter. I love you.'

'Then I wish you would show it rather more. Why don't you trust me? You've got nothing to worry about. Can't we just leave it at that? You've always got to have something to worry about. I just wish you wouldn't make it my secretaries, because that makes me angry.'

'Alan —'

'Do we have to talk? The sooner we get to sleep the sooner breakfast will be.'

'You'll never really discuss anything, will you? I want to talk about everything and you want to keep silent about everything.

Just suppose I was unfaithful to you, what would you do?'

'You have a great gift for forgetting things.'

'That was different, that was a long time ago. We were apart, of our own free wills, and it didn't count. But in general terms, if husbands get interested in other women, wives are supposed to be tactful and silent and not make scenes, and put on new corsets and get their hair done, and win their straying spouses back by patient loving endeavour. Now if *I* had a lover, would you try and win me back by behaving with restraint? Would you buy me roses and wash your feet and have your toe-nails manicured to please me better? Like hell you would!'

'What are you talking about now?'

'Just that there's one law for husbands and another for wives.'

'Of course there is. Wives need husbands more than husbands need wives.'

'What a terrible thing to say.'

'It is not terrible, it is simply true. Such is the structure of our society that women without husbands are scorned, and men without women admired. Provided they are known to be heterosexuals, of course. I notice an increasing tendency in women to label any unmarried man a queer, however; and to put about the damaging rumour that the fornicator is merely over-compensating, announcing to the world his sexual inadequacy. The male-female war is hotting up.'

'You are being flippant. It is not fair.'

'Of course it is not fair.'

'I wish I had been born a man.'

'You make that very apparent.'

'Now you are being unpleasant. Men are always accusing women of being unfeminine, and at the same time making sure that the feminine state is as unendurable as possible. You leave your dirty socks around for me to pick up. And your dirty pants. It's my place to pick them up, because I'm a woman. And if I don't, you accuse me of being unfeminine. It's my place to clean up your cigarette ash from the coffee cup where you've ground out your cigarette. I am only fit to serve you and to be used and to make your life pleasanter for you, in spite of such lip service as you may pay to equal rights for women. You may *know* that I am equal, with your reason, but you certainly don't *feel* that I am.'

'Quite the suffragette.'

'And that is still the worst term of abuse a man can think of to say to his wife.'

'I wouldn't like to see you join the ranks of the crusading women, I admit. It wouldn't make you any happier, and it is so unrestful.'

'You are so patronising. I hate men.'

'Ah, there we have it at last.'

'I don't hate you, personally. Only your race.'

'Don't worry too much about me. I'll survive. And you of course are free to go your own way.'

'You sound remarkably like Gerry, these days.'

'Thank you very much.'

'It is not altogether an insult. He is quite attractive in some ways.'

'He is a pompous bore.'

'He is very sexy.'

'He likes *young* girls, dear.'

'I am not as old and ugly as you think.'

'I don't think anything of the kind.' Alan sounded weary. 'You are a married woman with a grown-up child. Why can't you behave like one? You make yourself ridiculous with this kind of talk.'

'I feel hungry. I am all stirred up inside. I feel the way I did when I was eighteen. I don't know what I want but it's not this. I don't want to be this person, I don't want to be trapped in this body, in this house, in this marriage.'

'Thank you very much. You say the sweetest things.'

'Oh, let's go to sleep.'

'There's steamed fish tomorrow.'

'Charming,' she said. 'Life is so full of thrills.'

Alan, feeling that sleep was further than ever, got out of bed and stood upon the scales. He balanced from one foot to another to try and make the reading as low as possible. Proving to his own satisfaction that he had lost two pounds he said to Esther, 'There is something, however, that I haven't told you. If I have been behaving a little strangely, there is a reason for it.'

Esther opened her eyes, alarmed.

'My agent rang up last week,' he said. 'He likes my novel. He thinks it's going to make quite a splash. He's sent it to the publishers with a very strong recommendation. A pity you haven't read it. I would have liked to have discussed it with you.'

'Isn't that marvellous,' said Esther faintly. 'Isn't that wonderful! Why didn't you tell me earlier? We could have celebrated.'

'I didn't like Alan writing that novel,' said Esther to Phyllis. 'I didn't like it one little bit. And I liked it even less when he said his agent was enthusiastic.'

'I would have been proud,' said Phyllis. 'I'd think it was marvellous if Gerry could only do a thing like that. I wish

99

I'd married a writer. Writers stay at home most of the time. I could learn how to type and be a great help to him in his work.'

'I had no urge whatsoever to help Alan,' said Esther. 'Not in this respect. He'd come home from the office and have dinner and go into the bedroom and take out his typewriter and that would be that for the evening. I could sit staring into space for all he cared. And what would he have done if I'd gone off by myself and typed in the evenings? He wouldn't have stood for it. That's another of the rules of marriage. Husbands can snub wives but wives aren't allowed to indulge themselves in artistic endeavours: wives can only do so in secret, when husbands are out of the house. Wives are a miserable lot. I shall never be a wife again.'

'I think you should see a doctor. It's not right to think like that. It's perfectly natural for women to be wives, and to look after husbands who are not really fit to look after themselves, and it was very unfair of you to try and stop him writing. And most unwise. No wonder he looked elsewhere.'

'You have this extraordinary passion for simplifying things, Phyllis. I didn't try and stop him writing. I encouraged him. He was doing it just to annoy, anyway; to prove to me what a creative person he was and to demonstrate how I had stifled his talents and his personality. I knew from the way he would gobble down his dinner, pretending not to notice what he was eating, and then stand in the doorway and say, with his papers clutched in his hand – "I am going away to write now. I do not want to be disturbed –". He used such a challenging tone of voice that I quickly recognised the whole thing as an act of aggression. And he waited and waited for me to ask him

100

what it was about, and I wouldn't, so he had to go on writing and almost before he knew what had happened, he had finished. So he ought to have been grateful to me. Instead, he preferred to believe he had done it all in spite of me, and not to spite me, as was the truth.'

'Didn't you want to know what he was writing? I would have died of curiosity.'

'If he wanted it to be a secret, why should I bother?'

'Poor Alan! Trampling on his creativity like that.'

'Poor Alan, indeed. When did Alan ever do anything except exactly what he wanted when he wanted?'

'Well that's men, isn't it?'

'You do reduce everything to a kind of comic-strip level, don't you? All this happened the night before Gerry called.'

Phyllis paused in the careful peeling of an apple.

'Gerry?'

'Yes. Didn't he tell you?'

'He didn't mention it.'

'It was quite a casual visit. Perhaps he thought it wasn't important – oh, don't look like that, Phyllis. You don't own the poor man.'

'I don't want to own him. I just want not to be hurt by him. I want it to be like it was when I was a child, when you thought the day you got married you lived happily ever after. Esther, I'm cold. You talk and talk and none of it matters and then you say something and it's real. Turn on the fire.'

Phyllis tossed the unbroken strip of peel from her apple into the air. It curled to make a 'C' on the floor.

'C. I wonder who that is? I wonder who in the world that is. Do you think I will ever meet someone who will make me happy? I wouldn't mind waiting until I was seventy. Just so long as some day I do.'

'Men don't make women happy. Men make women unhappy.'

Esther crouched in front of the gas-fire, making toast.

'Gerry used to make me happy. I was so very happy once,' said Phyllis.

'It is the memory of past happiness that makes the present so intolerable. Better never to be happy at all.'

'Tell me about Gerry. What did he say? Why did he visit you? What happened? Did you let him make love to you?'

Esther turned to stare at Phyllis in an unsmiling way, and the toast burned.

Brenda now lay on the bed in her nightgown with her hands clasped behind her head and an expression of beatitude on her face that quite tormented Susan.

'Did you really let that man make love to you?' asked Susan. 'Just like that? A foreigner? A pick-up in a pub?'

'Yes. Why not? Why are you so interested? What more do you want to know? I don't like discussing clinical details. He was no different from an Englishman, really. There is no need to go on about his being a foreigner.'

'I don't understand how you can take such a thing so lightly.'

'You think you are the only person who ever feels anything. Who knows, perhaps he and me will get married.'

Susan looked at the prostrate figure on the floor. His watch was solid gold; his clothes must have cost a fortune in Carnaby Street; he had the smooth and silky skin of the protein-fed.

'You don't know his name,' she said. 'Or his income.'

'It doesn't matter. I feel I am in love. I have never been in love before. I want to feel like this for ever. My kind of love is not yours. Mine makes me happy. You say that that is being a whore. I think it's just being a normal, natural woman.'

'I think it's being a normal, natural man, more like. I think you have been born a boy.'

'My mother wanted me to be a boy. I am glad I am a woman, though, now. I feel wonderful.'

'You were feeling something quite different before. You were all anxious and worried.'

'When you came in looking so cross I felt I ought to apologise. The least I could do was not have enjoyed it. But now I am bored with pretending. I feel marvellous. I feel powerful. I think all I have to do is stretch out my little finger and men will fall down in front of me in droves. Do you ever feel like that?'

'Sometimes. Not often.'

'When I look back at the past I seem to have been so foolish. I worried about whether men would like me. But it doesn't matter, does it? What matters is whether I like them. What a revelation! Isn't life wonderful? I wonder what my mother would say. She'd have a fit.'

'She's probably in bed with the butcher at this very minute. Suburban widows are a randy lot.'

Brenda sat up.

'You have no right to say a thing like that. My mother loved my father very much and hasn't looked at a man since he died. She is a very good woman, and my father treated her very badly, which was what she wanted I'm afraid. She had to struggle very hard to bring me up, which she loved doing, and granted she isn't very intelligent, but she's a good woman, and very brave in the face of adversity – everyone says so; and the butcher is about eighty anyway. And I'll tell you another thing. I'm tired of being patronised by you. I don't think you know as much about love as you pretend. You may be kinky for artists and married men, but that doesn't mean you know everything about life.'

'Just because you've fallen into bed with a strange Asiatic and liked it doesn't mean you do, either. It was very unwise of you. I don't see him going down well in your family circle.'

'I won't really marry him. I will love him but never marry him, because East and West can never meet. He might be a Muslim, anyway, and his attitude to women not acceptable.'

'I hardly imagine he had marriage in mind when he followed you home from the pub. On a union lasting not more than a quarter of an hour at the very most.'

'You make everything sound so sordid. We'll see when he wakes. I think your relationship with William is sordid, taking a man away from his pregnant wife. And you and Alan, that was sordid too. Fancy fancying a man because he'd written a book! I feel too happy to be really angry with you, however. You only say nasty things because you're jealous: because I have some capacity for happiness and you have none. I feel liberated. I thought I would have to marry a bank clerk or a doctor or a solicitor and have children and be a housewife, but now I see I needn't do any of these things. I shall never get married.'

'You will have to.'

'Why?'

'Children. You want children.'

'You don't have to be married to have children.'

'You'll grow old and ugly. Then you'll need to be married.'

'*You* don't mean to get married. Why should it be different for me?'

'Because you have a suburban soul.'

'I have not. Didn't I just go to bed with him? Is that being suburban?'

'Yes.'

'Oh.' Brenda's look of happiness died. 'You can't win, can you,' she said in a small voice. She turned her head on to the pillow and began to cry.

'Now what's the matter?' asked Susan.

'I'm all upset inside. I don't know what's the matter. Is there enough hot water for a bath?'

'Yes.'

'It won't make any difference though. I'll still feel sticky and horrible.'

'That's just guilt.'

106

'Why should I feel guilty?' Brenda stopped crying to enquire.

'Because you're not married, and you don't love him, and you don't want his children.'

'Do you have to want someone's children not to feel guilty about making love to them?'

'Yes.'

'You didn't want Alan's children.'

'Good God, no.'

'Then?'

'But then I didn't like Alan in bed either. I wasn't really interested in bed, just his creative soul.'

Brenda got out of bed and knelt beside it and prayed.

'What on earth are you doing?'

'Praying.'

'To whom, for God's sake?'

'I don't know. Anyone.'

'What are you praying?'

'I'm just saying, "Dear God what shall we do to be saved?"'

'You are right to ask. I'll go away and leave you to your devotions.'

'Please don't. Don't go away until he does. If I shut my eyes, will you wake him up and get rid of him so that when I open my eyes he's gone?'

'Are you talking to me or to God?'

'You.'

Susan crossed to the sleeping man and kicked him. He grunted and stirred but he did not wake up. He was too drunk.

Esther scraped the toast into the sink. She looked with distaste at the black crumbs, and ran the tap to wash them away.

'I don't really eat,' she remarked. 'I scavenge. I am trying to clear up the mess that surrounds me, like a cat cleaning up after having kittens. Sometimes they eat the kittens too, by mistake.'

'You say horrible things,' said Phyllis, taking out her compact and staring at her face. 'Human beings are more than animals. I think you say these things just to shock me. But I am not easily shocked.'

'Where is Gerry now, do you think? At this very moment?'

'I don't know.'

'Why won't you answer my question?'

'It was an unworthy question.'

'What do you imagine Gerry is doing at this very minute? Let a vision come into your mind. I know what you see. You see him in bed with a woman. You don't know what she looks like, all you know is she isn't you. Perhaps she looks like me? Vaguely? He's just a vague shape too, isn't he? Your husband. You don't really believe he exists separately from you. At least I just eat food. You'd eat him, if you could. To incorporate him. That's a terrible way to be.'

'What are you talking about? I don't think Gerry is with another woman. And what horrible nonsense is all that other about eating him? What do you think I am? A cannibal?'

'You are shocked, aren't you. The truth is always shocking.'

'You're mad. What happened when Gerry came to see you?'

'What happened? What happened? Sexually? That's the only kind of happening you recognise. No wonder you fear growing old so much. But behaving and feeling as if you were fifteen won't stop your backbone shrivelling and your teeth falling out.'

'What happened? I begin to think you have something to hide.'

'Begin? You've been in a state of agitation ever since I said. Gerry came to see me. Nothing happened, in the sense you mean.'

'I'm sorry to be silly. It's just he always fancied you. I don't know why. He'd go mad if I put on a pound, yet he liked you.'

'He came to let me know, on the excuse of passing by, that he had seen Alan lunching with Susan in Soho, and to tell me, under guise of denigrating her, just how young, beautiful, slim and intelligent she was.'

'But why would he do a thing like that?'

'Why do you think?'

'He's horrible! He's always fancied you. He thought you'd pay Alan out in his own coin.'

'You might be wrong. Perhaps it was all quite innocent. Perhaps he *was* just passing by. Perhaps he *did* think I knew about Susan having lunch with Alan. Perhaps he hoped for nothing at all. Perhaps it is all just in our minds, and not in his. We must be careful not to mistrust all men, just because they are our enemies.'

'You are so confusing. I know Gerry was after you, but I don't think men are my enemies. I like men.'

'So do I. But I don't think women should have anything more to do with men than they can possibly help. They should not try and ape them, either. I wish you would not wear trousers, Phyllis.'

'I like wearing trousers.'

'Women should aspire to be as different as possible from men. You should wear a skirt as a matter of principle. There must be apartheid between the sexes. Men and women should unite only for the purpose of rearing children. Any woman who struggles to be accepted in a man's world makes herself ridiculous. It is a world of folly, fantasy and self-indulgence and it is not worth aspiring to. We must create our own world. I will lend you a skirt, Phyllis.'

Phyllis shuddered in spite of herself.

'We were talking about your husband,' said Esther, 'on whose account you make yourself so wretched. I am not sorry for you on this account, since you married him with the full intention of being wretched. I will tell you the truth. Your husband came round and made a pass at me, although I am all of fourteen stone and five years older than him. Now why did he do a thing like that?'

'What did you do? Esther!' Poor Phyllis was trembling.

'I?' said Esther. 'What would a woman like me do when a man like that makes a pass at her? "I like", he said to me, "a woman I can get my teeth into". To which I replied, "I am not normally a mass of toothmarks". That was quite witty, don't you think?'

'You're mad,' said Phyllis. She was standing up, pulling at her wedding ring, with her eyes so bright it was clear she was going to cry. 'You shouldn't talk to me about my husband like that. For pity's sake stop teasing me and tell me what happened. You are so clever and I am very stupid but it's not my fault. Please tell me!'

'I have already told you. Nothing happened that was of any account.'

'But what do you mean, "was of any account"? For all I know you'd go to bed with the Prime Minister and still say it wasn't "of any account".'

'Well, you know Gerry. It's all talk with him, isn't it.'

Phyllis started to cry. Mascara ran down her cheeks.

'Don't get hysterical,' said Esther. 'You wanted to hear this story. It's not my fault if it turns out to be something you don't want to hear.'

'Just tell me, Esther. I won't hold it against you.'

'Gerry and I did not make love,' said Esther, allowing Phyllis to see that her fingers were crossed. 'That night,' she added for good measure. 'Try and calm down, Phyllis. Why should you worry either way? What possible difference can it make to us, here and now, what happened to me a month or so ago? What matters is that your husband tried to upset me and succeeded.'

'All you can think of is yourself.'

'That is a charge that can fairly be levelled at every one of us. I wish you didn't have such trivial problems, Phyllis. You must learn to look outside them. Gerry's infidelity is merely a convenient hook on which to hang your anxieties. You would be better off as a peasant woman tilling the soil and trying to keep her family from starvation. Give any woman time to think and she's miserable at once. It is time you took up good works, Phyllis.'

'But you left Alan because he was unfaithful.'

'That is a gross simplification.'

'Well you didn't leave him just because he made you go on a diet.'

'He didn't make me go on a diet. We decided to do it. He quite wilfully set about depriving me. I quite wilfully set about depriving him. We conspired together to break our marriage, in fact. I was less whole-hearted about it than him. I would have retracted if I could. I made peace-offerings. I tried to cook him omelettes in butter. He chose to see it as an act of aggression. He was determined not to be married to me any more.'

'I don't understand.'

'I will try and explain tomorrow. Don't worry about me and Gerry, it was all of no significance. You tempt me into being unpleasant to you, that's all. I am very tired. I want to go to sleep. You must go home, Phyllis, or to walk the streets if you are still determined to punish Gerry by staying out. Perhaps, who is to say, he does in fact have to work late in the office? The money you live on must come from somewhere.'

'I will see you tomorrow evening,' said Phyllis forlornly. 'You need me. You are going through a great crisis in your life.'

And she left the flat, found her way up the dark, broken steps, hailed a taxi and went home. Gerry was not there. She took four sleeping pills and lost consciousness.

# 2

The others slept badly. Esther was very sick at about four in the morning. A great mass of undigested food poured back out of her mouth into the lavatory basin: she could taste the different flavours as it passed. The soup, the toast, the curry, the cake, the nuts, the eggs, the fish fingers, the butter, the jam, the beans, the cake – the whole evening's intake reappeared in a spasmic flow. She had not realised that her stomach could contain so much. On the way back to bed, exhausted from retching to recover the last troublesome chunk of nut, she caught sight of her naked body in the mirror, and stopped to stare at the rolls of fat which swathed her body like a sari. She pulled the blankets over her – she had no sheets – and before going to sleep wondered if perhaps she had not gone too far? She had not really meant any of this to happen – as a child may feel who, setting light to a wastepaper basket to draw attention to himself, then has to watch his entire home go up in flames.

Susan woke at about two, afraid. She thought there was someone in the room. Then she was incensed because there wasn't. Somebody had obviously abandoned her. But who? She couldn't remember. She was lying on her back and found it difficult to breathe. She began to think she was immensely pregnant, and even when she moved her hands over her belly and found it flat as ever, she was not reassured. The feeling that there was a mountain beneath her breasts remained. The mountain, moreover, stirred and moved and heaved. William had thus once described his wife's pregnancy in a poem which he read aloud to Susan as they lay communicative after making love, and the image of the moving mountain still pursued her. Now, in the dark, Susan rolled up her eyes in anxiety: they peered into her brain and made her dizzy. She was pregnant. Something had gone wrong. She did not attribute her condition to a man – it had just happened. Or she had caught pregnancy like a disease from some other woman. Probably, through contact with William, from William's wife. She switched on the light, sat up, and felt more reasonable. 'I am Susan Pierce,' she told herself. 'Nothing is uncontrollable. Everything is controllable. There is nothing for me to be frightened of. I am not pregnant.' Now her reason was working again she felt quite lively. She wondered if perhaps women had a primitive group soul that linked them together. The pregnancy had been real enough; it had just turned out to be someone else's, that was all. Sympathy with her sex, she thought, could go too far. She must struggle against it.

In the next room Brenda slept voluptuously on the sofa dreaming of picnics in the grass, of elegant ruffled ladies and handsome peruked men: water tinkled from a fountain. A fish with her mother's face swam in the pool below. She lay on the grass and the earth moved to accommodate her limbs. She

116

woke: she could not quite remember where she was or who she was. Presently she turned on the light and got out of bed and stood blinking, barefooted, and dressed in a pale-blue checked nightgown with a frill around the neck. The light woke the man on the floor, and he scrambled to his feet. Brenda's body, quite of its own volition, for her mind had not yet caught up with the events of the evening, made a kind of melting move towards him. But he took two pound notes from his pocket, handed them to her, bowed politely, and left. Brenda went and had a bath. She felt too humiliated to so much as cry.

In the morning they were all themselves again. Phyllis cooked Gerry's breakfast, with her face carefully made up, and composed into careful non-accusing lines. He ate heartily, and kissed her goodbye, for which she was grateful. Esther made herself a breakfast of porridge from a tin and evaporated milk, kipper from a plastic bag, already buttered, three Heinz tins called 'Junior Bacon and Egg Breakfast', toast, butter, marmalade, and coffee, to strengthen her after her illness. Then she began to feel sick again. Susan ate an apple, and some milk, took up her brush and painted. Brenda slept until eleven, and then blamed Susan for not waking her in time for her work as a receptionist in a Public Relations firm.

'I'm sorry,' said Susan, 'but I thought that now you'd started a career as a call girl you would wish to give up your job.'

Brenda slammed the door and left, breakfastless.

All the same, they all went visiting that morning.

Esther went to visit a doctor; Phyllis went to visit Alan; Susan went to visit Peter; and Brenda rang up her mother and had lunch with her.

Esther's gynaecologist, when she went to see him, had changed. He was no longer the grey-haired respectable Englishman she remembered. He was bronzed, buoyant, slim-hipped, crew-cut, and wore a flowered shirt. The medical books that once had lined the walls had been swept away, and replaced by splodgy paintings.

'You've changed,' she said.

'One has to move with the times, Esther,' he said. 'These days London is a swinging city. Mini-skirted mothers give birth with cries of joy, not pain. Doctors – at any rate those not on the National Health – must train themselves to laugh, not commiserate. Now that we recognise that illness is self-induced, we must be brutal with our patients. The Medicine of Brutality is all the rage, and very profitable. *Erewhon* is upon us. The sick must go to prison and the criminals to hospital. What can I do for you? I warn you that many of my more elderly patients have transferred themselves elsewhere.'

'I was sick in the night,' said Esther, 'I am ill. Perhaps you should take it all away.'

'All what?'

'You know. Those parts inside me that I no longer use. I think

118

they have fallen into decay and are poisoning me. Why else should I feel so sick all the time?'

'Because you are sickening yourself. Have you looked at yourself in the mirror lately?'

'Yes. Last night.'

'Then I suspect that that is why you are here. It is your guilt you wish to have excised, not your reproductive organs.'

'My guilt?'

'At so abusing the body God gave you. Correction,' he said, 'the body your parents gave you. You can't *like* being so fat.'

'I prefer it to other things, like being hungry. But I did not come here to discuss my size. I have a pain low down, and I feel sick all the time.'

'You make me feel sick too.' Having said it he smiled, seeming quite pleased with himself. Esther, feeling that in so freely indulging his rudeness he had achieved a lifetime's ambition, warmed to him just a little. 'You will have to lose some weight or I don't give twopence, not only for your reproductive organs, but for your life.'

'I'll tell you something,' she said, 'I don't give twopence for my life either. All the same, I don't wish to spend what remains of it in a state of nausea. Do you suggest I take my problems elsewhere?'

119

'My dear Esther,' he said, 'take them where you will. Wherever you go they will go too. I am merely pointing out that you wilfully aggravate matters by being so fat, and have done so as long as I have known you. You were a pretty girl, but much enveloped by blubber.'

'You live your sex life once. I chose to live mine emblubbered, that's all. And it's too late now, anyway.'

'I know your insides well, Esther, physically at any rate, but I have never been able to put my finger on the root of your spiritual discontent. Correction. Neurotic disorder.'

'Some people would have been better never born. I am one of them.'

'That is a silly thing to say.'

'It is what I believe. I should never have been born. I should have lived for ever in my mother's womb, where everything was dark and timeless, and I had no dimensions, and could not be seen, or judged. My mother, rot her, soon put an end to all that. She forced me out into the world, and I find it as hard to forgive her for this as she does me for fighting to stay inside, and giving her a bad labour. Things better should surely come after things good. And this is the whole of my discontent, that they don't. Since the moment I first found myself in this chilly, dangerous world things have gone from bad to worse. When I say I should never have been born, don't contradict me. Time goes so quickly, too. It frightens me. Once, for me, time was the measure of growth. Now it is the measure of decay.'

'If you are worrying about wrinkles, I know an excellent cosmetic surgeon who can remove them. The eyelids can be tightened. That makes a lot of difference. There is nothing to be ashamed of in a woman wanting to go on looking young and attractive. Why not?'

'I came here to be cured of my sickness, not beautified. I don't care what I look like.'

'I have told you what to do. Stop sickening yourself.'

'Will you charge me for this consultation?'

'Most certainly.'

'But you haven't *done* anything.'

'My time is valuable, patients are queuing up to see me as they never used to when I was a more orthodox practitioner – and I have put up with your complaints.'

'I have friends to do that, free.'

'Oh yes. Mrs Frazer. I met her at dinner. I asked how you were and she replied, "Fat, and talkative". How is her bosom?'

'Bosom?'

'I assumed she would have told you. She went into considerable detail over the roast. She has had it lifted.'

'I didn't know she had any to lift.'

'That is not for me to say.'

'Crop the nose and lift the face,' said Esther. 'Tilt the breast and pin the ear – why do women do it?'

'To please men, I should think. All men, if they're in show biz. One man, if they are neglected wives.'

'It is a degrading sport, this beauty hunting. Worse than chasing foxes. Undignified both for the doctors who do it, and the women who indulge in it.'

'Dignity is out of date – just look at me! My trousers are so tight I can scarcely sit down, and I am off to the Bahamas tomorrow. And surely, if a husband fancies his wife big-breasted, and the wife obliges, then the sum of human happiness has been increased, has it not?'

'Human sensation perhaps. Human happiness, no.'

'Don't delude yourself, they are the same thing.'

'It is true that Gerry Frazer likes large women,' said Esther. 'Or at any rate he claims to. I wonder why he ever married someone as skinny as Phyllis?'

'The change in his tastes may well accord with the change in him. Being fat now himself, he does not wish to court criticism and unkind comparisons.'

'You are really quite acute,' she said, 'in a dismal kind of way. You never used to be.'

'It is more profitable like this. Had you realised that infertility is a psychic, not a physical state?'

'Nothing surprises me,' she said, 'except doctors.'

'Aggression and obesity go together,' he said, and she wished she had never left her basement.


Phyllis rang Alan's office and was told he was in bed with flu. She called to see him, and sat by his bed.

'Poor darling Alan,' she said, 'I had to come. All alone with no one to look after you. Now tell me, what can I do?'

'You can leave me alone,' he said, but he was grateful to see her.

'You and Esther, you're as grumpy as a pair of pigs. You just can't get on without each other.'

'You've seen Esther?'

'Yes. Yesterday. No thanks to you, hiding her address like that. What are you trying to do to her? She's in trouble and she needs all the help she can get. Don't you care what happens to her?'

'No.'

'You only say that. When you've been married as long as you two have, of course you care.'

'Caring may be a habit, but it is not necessarily a good habit.'

'You've behaved very badly, Alan; she's very hurt and upset. I know how terribly bad I'd feel if Gerry got involved with his secretary.'

He raised his eyebrows at her.

'Marriage is a very hurtful business, I know,' she said in a small voice. 'At least it is for me, but there's no reason for you and Esther to fight. And I know you think I've got a nerve, interfering, but I do honestly want to see you both happy again. I admire Esther so much. She's everything I'm not. She's clever, and she's grown up. And it breaks my heart to see her like this.'

'I give you credit for your good intentions. I am afraid I am somewhat rude. Times have been troublesome lately. Quite apart from anything else, the office bores me to hell, and Peter irritates me beyond belief. He has no idea of the seriousness of life: he is basically and deeply frivolous. It is Esther's fault. She bred cynicism in him. Wherever I look, I see nothing whatever to brighten my life.'

'There's your writing. That's a wonderful hobby to have. I wish Gerry was as clever as you.'

'Oh, yes,' he said with profound gloom, 'the novel.' He sank back into his pillows, as if struck by sudden feebleness. 'A hobby. Yes, I suppose that is what it was. How strange that I should have thought it to be the shaft of light which would illumine my whole life and give it meaning, and that in truth it is on a par with stamp-collecting and pigeon-fancying. There was a certain amount of confusion about the novel, to be frank. The agent attributed the wrong manuscript to me – the one he liked so much was written by a lady in Eccles. Mine, it turned out, he didn't like. It frightened him. He said it was cold and cruel and improper. Pornographic, even. I thought myself it was warm and friendly. How little one knows of oneself. Oh Phyllis, there must be something else in life than this?'

She was alarmed at such a question. 'Alan, I don't know what you're complaining about. You've got this divine home, and a clever wife who's a good cook, and a handsome clever son, and a good job and enough money, and why you suddenly want to spoil it all by taking up with a silly young girl who's just kinky for authors –'

'Who said so?'

'Esther.'

'Esther knows nothing about it.' He was cross.

'– because it's bound to upset everyone, isn't it? You should value what you've got and not go looking for something else all of a sudden. It's very immature of you. It's the way Gerry goes on, only he's like that all of the time, not just all of a sudden. And I can see you're upset about your novel, but people never do appreciate what's good, do they? The first thing you should do is go and ask Esther to come back. Then you can settle down again.'

'Why should I ask her back? She doesn't want to be here or she wouldn't have gone.'

'She's your wife.'

'You have this mystic faith in titles, Phyllis. It does you credit. No the home's broken up. Peter's gone. He lives during the week with crop-haired Stephanie. He's totally irresponsible and he expects me to pay his rent. He comes home at week-ends and sits doing his homework, and when he takes out his fountain pen packets of contraceptives fall out. He buys them with his pocket money. From a slot machine.'

'That's not irresponsible. That's responsible. He's a big boy now. He's a grown man. He's eighteen. It's not his fault if he's still at school. I expect he only does it to annoy you, anyway.'

'Perhaps he's not my son at all. How am I to know? I wasn't like that when I was his age. Only in my fantasies, not in real life.'

'Now you're being ridiculous.'

'Oh no I'm not. You don't know the half of it. There was a time in her life when Esther went mad. She cropped her hair, ate nothing but apples and went on the streets.'

'I don't believe you.'

'Well not quite the streets but the number of men visitors coming and going in her flat, it might as well have been the common pavement, and she lying in the gutter having it off with all and sundry.'

'Don't talk like that.'

'I'm sorry. Anyway, she calmed down and I accepted her back. But nothing she does surprises me any more. And why she should get in such a state because I like talking to my secretary and should so bitterly resent my feeble attempts to have a rewarding and pleasant relationship with another woman — it's not reasonable of her.'

'It didn't sound very platonic, the way Esther described it.'

'I never said it was platonic. But that was beside the point. Esther needed her freedom. When she got tired of it I had her back. I would have thought she could have afforded me the same courtesy and not left me here to die of influenza. I'll tell you another thing. Susan admired me. Esther never, in all her life, admired me. Esther is incapable of admiring a man.'

'She is so unhappy down there in her basement she would be ready to admire anyone.' Phyllis took off her little flowered hat and shook her curly hair free. 'And I'm sure she does admire you, Alan. How could anyone not? You're so clever and so good-looking. You have this kind of fine-boned sensitive face, and such deep eyes I think a woman could lose herself in them utterly. And you are so good at taking control of things. I do admire that in a man.'

'I suspect you,' said Alan. 'Why do you want Esther back here? Because of Gerry?'

She looked startled, and was too confused to reply.

'I know nothing about her and Gerry, mind you,' he went on, 'except I think Gerry must be out of his mind. Why can't he be happy with you? You're a proper feminine woman. I think the only one left in the entire world. You must excuse me. I feel weak. I have felt weak for a long time now. First it was lack of food, then it was lust, then it was literature, then it was Esther's hysteria, then Susan's neurotics, now it's flu. If it's not one thing it's another and it's a bit much. Everything suddenly boils over all at once, Phyllis, I am very weak and you are taking advantage of me.'

'Alan, what happened between Gerry and Esther?'

'So that's why you came to see me. Not because I was ill and not because you liked me but to get something out of me. I might have known. What difference does it make, Gerry and Esther, or Gerry and a dozen other women. None of it means a thing to him. One body or another, it's all the same.'

'Because Esther's my friend.'

'A fine friend. She'd sell you down the river a hundred times, the way she sold me. Why do you put up with Gerry? It's cold outside, Phyllis. Come into bed.'

Phyllis took off her flowered little-girl smock, and stood in her lacy stockings, her red brassiere and red suspender belt by the bed. She had put on her best underwear for the visit. Alan, his eyes bright and his brow fevered, lay back on the pillows and watched.

128

'Everyone else does,' said Phyllis miserably, 'why shouldn't I?'

'Quite so,' said Alan. 'Those are my feelings exactly.' She took off what remained of her clothes and climbed into bed, where she lay inert and shivering.

'You are very cold,' he said. 'It's rather refreshing to encounter a woman like you.'

'You are very warm,' she said. 'I wish I wasn't so miserable. Why does Gerry get so much pleasure from going to bed with other women? If you don't feel affectionately towards someone, there's no pleasure in it, is there? At least that's what the books say. Perhaps he just manages to feel affectionate towards lots and lots of people. I've never been to bed with anyone in my entire life except Gerry and I don't understand what all the fuss is about. I am a frigid woman, you see. Unless it is that I have never met the right man. You are welcome to any comfort I can give you,' she added, lying more stiffly than ever.

'Please, please feel affectionately towards me,' he moaned. 'Someone has to.'

She did indeed, at that, feel a flicker of affection.

'You said I was a proper feminine woman. What did you mean by that?'

'You are gentle and docile and slim and pretty and neat, like a doll. You endure things. You don't try to be anything, ever, except what you are. You have pretty little eyes that never see more than they should. You are not in the least clever and

129

you never say anything devastating. I should have married you.'

She began to feel quite cheerful.

'I even think I could make you happy,' he said, at which such feeling overwhelmed her that she turned towards him, and he clasped her, or rather clutched her, as if he was a drowning man and she the straw he sought for. She shut her eyes and pretended he was Gerry. There was very little difference between them, if she put her mind to believing it. She was pleased, anyway, to be the means of his pleasure, being grateful to him for his kind words. Afterwards a terrible thought occurred to her.

'You never actually *said* that Gerry and Esther made love.'

'No I don't suppose I did.'

'Did they?'

'I don't know and I don't care. Do you?'

'You led me to believe they had. I think you were plotting to get me into bed with you.'

He considered. 'It's possible.'

'That was despicable of you,' she pulled away from him so that she no longer touched him, and immediately felt bereft. She hoped he would move nearer to her, but he did not do so.

'I think it would be despicable of you to make love to me

'simply because you wanted to be revenged on your husband.'

'It's not much revenge,' she said, and sounded disappointed. 'It doesn't add up to much, does it. People talk and talk about it, but in itself it's such an unimportant thing.'

He felt his temperature rising. He began to shiver.

'You bloody women,' he said, 'you're all the same. You're never satisfied.'

She got out of bed and dressed. He did not watch her. His head ached.

'It's not your fault,' she said, charitably, when she felt respectable again and had sprayed herself with scent. 'It's me. I'm frigid, you see. I was only trying to help you, and cheer you up. And really I enjoyed it very much.'

'I'm not a cream tea,' he groaned.

'We shouldn't really have done it,' she went on. 'How can I look Esther in the eye? I'll never be able to see her again, and I'm supposed to be calling this afternoon. Oh what will I do? What have I done?'

'Next time,' was all he said, 'please choose another man to inflict your frigidity upon.'

She cried, and said, 'I thought love was meant to make people happy. I was only trying to help.'

❏

'Of course,' said Peter to Susan, 'Father is very upset. He is insanely jealous of me. It is often a problem when middle-aged men see their sons grow up and begin to have sex lives, and with Father the experience is proving quite traumatic. Apart from the length of your hair, you see, you are remarkably like Stephanie; who, again, is like my mother in her thinner moments. I think this was what attracted him to you in the first place. If I can sleep with Stephanie, why couldn't he sleep with you? It was unfortunate that Mother took it so seriously. If she had had any insight she would have understood him, and stayed, and waited for it to blow over. But again, when sons leave home, women tend to despair. What is there left for them? I am afraid the whole thing is my fault. Men have a menopause too, did you know? I think Father is suffering from it. Why exactly did you feel you had to come to see me?' He was dressed in black from head to foot. He was doing his homework. His school-books lay open on the purple velvet settee.

'Because I didn't want you to hold any of this against me. When two people fall in love it quite often happens that someone gets hurt. It is one of the tragedies of living.'

'Why should you care what I think?'

'Because you're of my own generation, I suppose.' Her long legs were crossed and she smoked a cigarette from a holder. Her nails were long and beautifully manicured.

'It's extraordinary,' he said, 'how like Stephanie you are. You would have made a smashing stepmother. In an incestuous kind of way.'

132

'I think that thought occurred to your father,' she said. 'It troubled him. It was one of the reasons –'

He looked doubtful. 'Did you really get as far as that? I don't think he really ever contemplated divorce. Men don't break marriages lightly. That's one of the reasons I'm not married to Stephanie. That, and me being at school. Have I said something wrong? You're looking all miserable.'

'Oh no,' she said, 'it's all right. It's just I take things seriously and I don't understand how other people can't. I am an artist, you see, and everything appears more real to me than it does to other people. And being more real is more painful. Your father found reality painful too, I think. He is a very sensitive person, in many ways, but confused, I suppose. You are very like him, but you have not been maltreated and twisted by life, as he has. You don't think women are things, do you? You believe they are people, don't you?'

'Of course.' He looked surprised. 'Didn't he?'

'No, not really. It is a common complaint with men of his generation. I keep having to batter away at their impregnability. It's a kind of compulsion. It never works. They still think I'm just a piece of decoration on a birthday cake, and get very angry if I so much as open my mouth to say anything except how marvellous they are. That's what I like about artists and poets and painters. They believe women are people. They don't mind getting hurt. I don't mind getting hurt, either. Your father hurt me.'

'I don't know why you take him so seriously. He's so old.'

'He's very fond of you. He thinks the world of you. That's because you look so much like him. He's a very good-looking man, you know. And very clever. But it's all no use. He's been destroyed by years of petit-bourgeois living: after all he's an ad-man. You'll never be an ad-man, will you?'

'I certainly hope not.'

'Because it destroys the soul, doesn't it? Your father says you write poetry. Can I see some?'

'I'd be delighted,' he said, blushing. 'You're a friend of William Macklesfield's, aren't you? He's one of my heroes. Poetry seems so simple when he writes it. So familiar, somehow.'

'He's a family man,' she said, not without bitterness. 'All the same, I know him well. I think I contribute something to his work. I wish I was more of a family woman. I get very tired of living the way I do, sometimes.'

'Perhaps you've never met the right man?' He was eager. 'I mean honestly, Dad wouldn't be right for you at all. He's much too old, and anyway he's married to Mother, so how could he have a whole-hearted relationship with you? I'm sure he would have if he could have, but being married, how could he? You mustn't let it upset you. You're not like Stephanie; she doesn't get upset by anything. I don't think that's right in a woman. I get the feeling I'm being used, if a girl's too cheerful about things. One welcomes a little intensity; I mean it's easy to be intense about politics, but a girl should be intense about sex too, to my way of thinking. I think the better of you for being upset, really I do.'

'All the other men I've met,' she said, 'only like me when I'm laughing. If I cry they go away. I suppose if one was married they wouldn't be able to so much. It is very refreshing to meet a man who doesn't mind one being miserable. Perhaps it's because you're so young. As you grow older and feel more like crying yourself you may be less well able to bear it.'

He put his arm around her, conscious that here his father's arm had been before him. He kissed her forehead.

'What about Stephanie?' she asked. 'I don't want to cause any more trouble. I'm older than you. I ought to be responsible.'

'She understands,' he said, steering her towards the couch. 'She is not at all possessive. All she ever does is laugh and cut her hair. Anyway she doesn't get back from work until seven. I get back from school at half past four, unless there's games. I'm in the school cricket team. It's a frightful bore but one can't let them down.'

'Thank God,' she said, succumbing, 'thank God you're not married. I can't stand married men. I can't stand competing with their wives.'

Under his weight, the unwanted gift pregnancy that still haunted her was beautifully flattened out, like a steak under a meat mallet. She pretended he was William Macklesfield. There was very little difference between them, if she put her mind to it. She was pleased, anyway, that someone so young, so handsome, so much his father's son, should afford her so much pleasure.

'You're not doing this,' he asked anxiously, 'to be revenged on my father or anything?'

'Revenged? Why should I want to be revenged?'

'Because he didn't take you seriously.'

'You've got it all wrong,' she said, 'it was I who didn't take him seriously.' And she crept under him again as if to hide.


'If you ask me,' said Brenda's mother, cutting through a *mille feuille* with a silver cake fork in the tearooms at the top of Dickens and Jones, 'inside your friend Susan, struggling to get out, is a dumpy little woman in a check apron with a rolling pin in the pocket. It is the only thing about her which reconciles me to your sharing that flat. And of course the knowledge that you are a sensible girl and aren't going to do anything silly. It is all talk with your friend Susan, all this sex and emancipation and art. It is quite obvious she just wants to be married but no one will ask her so she has to make do with free love. Who would want a girl like that, anyway?'

'Oh Mother,' said Brenda desperately, staring round the tables where well-dressed, middle-aged ladies with crocodile shoes and becoming hair-styles nibbled and sipped. 'Everything is so different nowadays. You don't understand.'

'Nothing changes. Women want to get married and have babies just as they always did. But your generation hasn't got the self-discipline ours had. My life with your father wasn't all roses, but I didn't complain. I stuck it out and I was very sorry when he died.'

'Well, his salary cheque stopped coming, didn't it. That was really the only difference I noticed. We never saw him.'

'Now why should you say a thing like that? London life makes you very rude. I don't imagine young men have changed so much since my day that they appreciate rudeness in a girl.'

'But Mother I don't much care what men think of me. No, don't look like that. I'm not a Lesbian, it's all right. I just think it's as important what I think of men as what they think of me.'

'Well it's not, is it? Women have always tried to make themselves attractive to men, and you're not going to change a thing like that in a hurry. Look around you. All the women nicely groomed and attractive and good-looking, and the men no better than fat slugs, for the most part, or skinny runts. Unshaved and smelly as often as not. They get away with everything, men. They can do every disgusting thing they like and no one ever says a thing. Today is the seventh anniversary of your father's death.'

Her voice had risen, embarrassing Brenda, and there was a mad look in her eye with which Brenda was familiar, and with which she had lived for many years, and which was likely to lead to broken mirrors and china and her mother lying on her back raving amidst the debris. So the daughter, who never really gave up hope of extracting some soupçon of wisdom and enlightenment from the mother about the nature of true love, decided that now was not the time to seek it. She changed the subject to cream cakes and after tea they went down to the underwear department on the third floor and bought see-through nighties and frilly suspender belts for each other.

Presently Phyllis overcame her scruples sufficiently to visit Esther again. Esther lumbered to the door in her dressing-gown and having let Phyllis in, retreated back to bed.

'I am feeling rather sick,' she said.

'I am not surprised,' said Phyllis.

'Everyone says that. The trouble is, if I stop eating I feel even sicker than I do if I don't stop eating. I will have to learn to live with nausea, I suppose. I have done you a great wrong, Phyllis.'

'What do you mean? What have I done?' asked Phyllis, mis-hearing.

'You have done nothing. What are you feeling so guilty about? I have wronged you by trying to stop you grieving, by denying that you had any cause to grieve. You may grieve for all the wrong reasons, but grieve you do. Grief is a lovely word and a lovely thing. It heals, as resentment cannot. Grief must be admitted and lived through, or it turns into resentment, and continues to bother you for the rest of your life, rearing its depressed little head at all the wrong moments, so that one Sunday tea time at the old lady's home you will unexpectedly begin to cry into your toasted teacake, and the nurses will say "Poor Mrs Frazer, that's the end", and will move you into the senile ward, when the truth of the matter is quite different. It's not senility, but grief grown uncheckable with age. Myself, I cry now and eat now, so as not to cry later, when it is yet more dangerous. I shall make a very cheerful old lady.'

'You're feeling better today then,' said Phyllis.

'Better in my mind but sicker in my body. I am angry with you.'

Phyllis turned pale. 'Why?'

'It has come to my notice that you had your breasts enlarged.'

'I didn't want you to know. Not enlarged, anyway. Tiptilted, is more like it.'

'Why did you keep it from me?'

'You're so odd about some things. I've done nothing to be ashamed of.'

'You ought to be ashamed. It was a degrading thing to do. To allow your body to be tampered with by a man, for the gratification of a man, conforming to a wholly masculine notion of what a woman's body ought to be. That you, a decent woman, should offer yourself up as a martyr to the great bosom-and-bum mystique; should pander to the male attempt to relate not to the woman as a whole, but to portions

139

of the female anatomy; should be so seduced by masculine values that you allow your breasts to be slit open and stuffed with plastic. They are, let me remind you, mammary glands, milk producers.'

'Sometimes you are quite disgusting.'

'The truth is always disgusting to people like you. On the day you let that happen to you, Phyllis, you become less of a woman, for all your brand new bubbly bosom. Didn't it hurt?'

'Yes.'

'Serve you right.'

'I don't understand your attitude at all. I like to look nice. My clothes look better for a bit of bosom. And anyway you're always saying how awful it is to be a woman.'

'Never! It would be perfectly acceptable being a woman if only men didn't control the world. If only it were possible to accept their seed to create children, yet feel obliged neither to accept their standards nor their opinion of womankind, which is, let's face it, conditioned by fear, resentment and natural feelings of inferiority.'

'It's better when you eat than when you talk.'

'Why haven't you and Gerry got any children?'

Phyllis wondered whether perhaps Alan had made her pregnant, and decided, for no rational reason, that he had not.

'That wasn't an attack,' said Esther, 'I simply wondered. There is no reason for a woman to have children if she doesn't want to. But if your reason for not is the preservation of your figure for Gerry's benefit then I shall, indeed, think the less of you for it.'

Phyllis blushed, which made her look very pretty.

'Do you intend to go on like this for ever,' asked Esther, 'spending your entire life attempting to placate that fat selfish bully of a husband?'

'I love my husband. It's a pity you don't love yours a little more, letting him lie there ill with flu. You can talk and talk about woman's rights, but it doesn't seem to make you very happy. And you tease me about everything, and you won't even tell me about you and Gerry. It's not fair.'

'Nothing happened between me and Gerry. I sent him home.'

Phyllis was put out by this news, hoping now for Esther's misbehaviour to justify her own.

'I've only ever been to bed with Gerry,' she said.

'I went mad once,' said Esther. 'It was very interesting. I got very depressed after my father died and drank a bottle of bleach. It didn't kill me but I couldn't swallow for months and I got quite thin, and I left Alan to find out what the world was like – and do you know what? It was full of men. So I went back to Alan. And do you know what? Alan's no different from all the others. You live with them for years, you clean and cook for them, you talk to them, you listen to them, you share your children with them, and you achieve nothing. They are still apart from you, suspicious of you, wishing and wishing you could be a piece of docile flesh, no more. Juliet was trying to tell me that, I think. She didn't mind about it. She didn't expect anything else. But we middle-class women are brought up with notions of partnership in marriage and that's why we all go mad and end up in bed with the plumber. It's time to get on with the story.'

# 3

On the twelfth day of the diet Esther sat at her kitchen table and drank black coffee. Her head was dizzy and her hands trembled. Juliet sat opposite her and cleaned a copper saucepan, after a fashion.

'You've got to give them a good time haven't you,' said Juliet. 'You can't grudge them their rights. They've got a right to expect certain things. You-know-what, and a hot meal when they come home from work. That keeps them quiet, and they don't interfere. What more do you want?'

'It's not as easy at that.'

'You haven't got enough to do that's your trouble. You let things get on top of you. I'm sorry for the husbands in all the houses I do for. All these *thoughts* going on around them all the time. I'm never idle, that's what it is. I'm always at it.'

'There doesn't seem anything to do any more, except fill in time. Once I had a garden but I filled it in with concrete because it was neater, and because I just didn't seem able to grow things any more. I'd lost my touch.'

'You're not as young as you were. I mean, who of us is?'

'My world is so small. My body is shrivelling. Perhaps that's why I need to be fat.' She held out her arm for Juliet to see. 'You see? I am used to seeing my arm as it was when I was young – it was white and firm. Now it is greyer, and flabby. I am going to die, Juliet.'

'Aren't we all? I don't know what the fuss is about. You should do a little more, think a little less. I'm never idle, that's my secret. I'm always busy.'

Esther raised her eyebrows in disbelief, and unfortunately Juliet saw.

'I should eat a biccy if I was you. It's silly, starving yourself like this.'

'I've lost ten pounds.'

'That's not much, is it. For a person your size. You could never tell. I hope you don't mind me saying so, but you could just never tell.'

'You could do with a bit off yourself, Juliet.'

'The difference between you and me is, of course, that I've never had any trouble with boys. If you start off popular you don't really care ever after. It didn't seem to matter what I looked like, they were always there, queuing up. I don't suppose it was like that for you, what with your size and all.'

'I don't do too badly, thank you, Juliet.'

Juliet held the saucepan under the tap, rubbed at it with Brillo, and talked over her shoulder to Esther.

'I can't seem to shift the stains on this pan. I think it's finished, Mrs Sussman, I really do. It needs throwing out.'

'No,' said Esther, with some passion. 'It is not finished.'

'All right. All right.'

'Old things ought to be cherished and looked after.'

'Throw them out. No use to anyone. Old ugly pans are like old ugly people. Once the children are grown up, they're no use to anyone.'

'Children always need their parents.'

'What, your Peter? He doesn't need anyone. Except a vicar to get him married. He's off now, anyway.'

'Off? What do you mean?'

'Your Peter. Sharing with Stephanie.'

'What are you talking about?'

'I heard him on the phone. Didn't he tell you? He's going to share that girl's flat. If she is a girl, with that hair. I don't mean to worry you, but I should find out. You can't have him growing up a poof, can you.'

'Of course he told me,' lied Esther, her hands trembling even more. 'I don't know that it will come to anything, though. You know what children are, making plans.'

'Children!' said Juliet. 'I don't think you've taught him proper respect for women, that's the trouble. You'll be a grandmother any minute if you're not careful, six times over in the same month.'

'You're exaggerating.'

'A big boy like that, it's very unsettling in the house. The sooner he's on his own the better. For you, and Mr Sussman too. It puts ideas in the head, somehow.'

'I dare say.'

'This house is getting like a morgue. You can feel it when you come in through the door. It gives me the shivers.'

'I always used to bake in the mornings. Everything used to smell nice and homely. But it's wrong to cook. It makes us fat. Nothing I do is much use to anyone, is it?'

'Well, you said it, not me.'

Esther's hand crept out to the plate of biscuits which had been put out for Juliet. Then she drew it back.

'You don't even nag much any more,' said Juliet. 'You'll lose your standards and then where will you be? What'll you have left then?'

Esther's hand reached for the biscuit again. This time it got there. She put the biscuit to her lips. Juliet whirled round.

'I saw you! I'll tell him! I'll tell him what you've been up to. I saw you!' She was half-joking, half-malevolent.

'Get out of my house,' said Esther.

'But I haven't finished yet.'

'Get out of my house and don't come back,' said Esther, who after all had said too much to Juliet, and having distorted the balance of the relationship, now had no option but to finish it completely. 'I'm sick of you and your insolence and your spying. I'll do the work myself. Coming here, taking advantage of me day after day, listening to me, mocking me. Taking my money, giving me nothing in return – nothing –'

She was by now pale with anger. Juliet carefully and slowly took off her apron, as someone who has won a long-sought victory, and left. When she had gone, Esther leaned her head on the table and cried. She rang Alan for comfort but was told he had not been in the office that day.

'I don't understand why you have such trouble with your staff,' said Phyllis. 'Mine always stay. Yours always get out of hand.'

'It's because I can never see why other people should do my dirty work, and so I am apologetic about it. Or else I talk too much. There are so few people to talk to. When I rang Alan to tell him how horrible Juliet was and found he wasn't there I wished Juliet was back again so I could tell her all about it.'

'Where was he?'

'Well where do you think he was? He was with that silly slut Susan.'

'What's the matter with you?' Susan asked Brenda with some impatience. Brenda, back from work, lay on her back on the bed instead of cooking dinner.

'I am in love. I was too tired before to notice but now I know I am. It is distinguished by a strange breathless feeling under the ribs; a kind of pattering fluttering of feeling. I suppose if one was pregnant and the baby kicked it would feel like that. It is not a very pleasant feeling but it is very important. I can see that it would lead one to do all kinds of drastic things, like murder and divorce. It will only ever be still when I lie in a bed with my arms around him.'

'Who do you happen to be in love with?'

'That man who was here last night. Why should I have this feeling about a man I can't even speak to? It is not the union of two minds. Could it be the union of two bodies? Susan, why did he give me two pound notes and not his telephone number?'

'Because that's what they charge. How was he to know the difference? He could only judge you on your actions. You had

148

no words to explain that you do not make a habit of such behaviour, if indeed you don't, which I am not in a position to know. Didn't you hand it back?'

'No. It was all too sudden. And I was grateful that he had given me something else. Besides himself, if you see what I mean. And then he was gone and I'm all upset and I want to see him again and if I don't I think I shall die. Tonight I will go to the pub and wait for him. I tried to talk to my mother but she had one of her mad fits in the middle of Dickens and Jones and I nearly died of embarrassment. What I don't understand is why I should feel like this about this man when I haven't about any of the others. Actually there were only two, to tell you the truth, they were both very suitable, chosen by my mother. Perhaps that's why I couldn't fancy them. And they talked too much. The more they talked the more I saw them for what they were and I despised them. Isn't that terrible?'

'I expect they were too nice to you. It's easier to love people when they're unpleasant to you. You are coming on, I must say. A little suffering will do you a world of good. Let's have a drink. I saw Alan's son today.' Susan confided this almost shyly.

'You didn't! You have got a nerve.' They drank their sherry with relish.

'Well it annoys me the way men will try to get you all totally involved and at the same time try and confine you to a tiny part of their lives. If you're involved, they should be involved too, it's only reasonable. I don't understand why Peter's turned out so marvellous with such screw-ball parents.'

'How is he marvellous?'

'He is lovely. He is so simple. He is divine. I always knew he would be. Alan kept his picture on his desk. He's only eighteen and already he lives with this girl. He's much too young for me. Such lack of complication is a bit overpowering but what a body. What a body. One could become hooked on mere flesh and bones – had you thought of that? But of course you have. It's your forte. Perhaps you are right and a silent man is the only truly desirable man there is. From now on, everything's going to be different.'

'I think it's horrible. It's like incest. First father, then son.'

'Not at all. I find I do hope he tells his dad, all the same. Is that horrible of me?'

'Yes. What happened between you and Alan to make you so angry?'

'I will tell you. Perhaps if I can get it straight in my mind it will stop me feeling so awful. Except I don't know if I'm feeling awful about Alan or about William. I didn't think I cared about William but I find I miss him. He was so good to talk to, and we got on so well, and we had so much in common, and I don't understand why that silly stupid cow of a wife of his should have him just because she breeds all the time. What is this magic in reproduction? One gets it all the time. My wife, my child. My child's birthday. My wife's birthday. Someone's ill. Someone's speech day. It's Christmas. It's Whitsun. All the time this bloody fucking father-child husband-wife obsession. Can't men just exist by themselves

150

for more than an hour at a time? Why do they have to have their appendages?'

'Then you shouldn't go with married men, should you?'

'You know what Peter's got? A cricket team. He hasn't got a wife. He hasn't got a child. But already, a cricket team. Sometimes I wish I was a Lesbian.'

'I've told my mother I wasn't a Lesbian. That's the worst fate she could imagine for me. Why do old people feel so strongly about these things?'

'It upsets them to think they may have lived their lives in error. That they could have had fun, and didn't. They had children instead.' She stood in front of the mirror, scraping back her blonde hair against her head, so that her cheekbones appeared bony and strong.

'Sometimes you remind me of a man.'

'Sometimes I feel like a man.'

'I wonder why my mother thinks there's a dumpy little hausfrau inside you trying to get out? I think it's more like a footballer.'

'What a horrible thing to say.'

'Which? The hausfrau or the footballer?'

'Both. I think such fantasies reflect badly upon both you and your mother. They say nothing about me – it simply indicates that your mother has Lesbian tendencies and that you are kinky for brutish men. We already have evidence for both these suppositions, of course.'

'I don't think I like sharing a flat with you. All I want is time to think about how I love this man, and someone to talk to about him, and all I get from you is cynical, complicated, upsetting talk.'

'You needn't think I like sharing a flat with you, either. I wish William was here. William is the only person who has ever understood and appreciated me.'

'Nobody,' said Alan, 'has ever really appreciated me.' He lay on his back on the bed on the thirteenth day of the diet; the same bed where later Brenda was to lie and suffer, in her headlong flight from reality, the pangs of true love. Susan was in her artist's smock and stood at the easel with a paintbrush in her hand. 'All my life nobody has ever really appreciated me. All my life I have been used. My mother used me; she would dress me up in the same spirit as she dressed her poodle, in a little fur coat and red bootees, and take me out for walks. If you have a dog you never lack friends, she would say. Bloody beast, it nearly bit my nose right off. It's never been the same. It has this bump in the middle. Deformed.'

'It seems a very straight nose to me.'

'Do you think so? It's a funny thing, Peter has this same bump in his nose. What do you think that proves?'

'That he's your son, I suppose.'

'I don't mean that, I mean it would either imply that that bloody animal didn't in fact damage my nose to the degree I have always believed, or that Lysenko was right.'

'Lysenko?'

'Inheritance of acquired characteristics. You are fairly ignorant of facts, if nothing else. You are probably wise to be so. My father used me as a repository for useless information. What is the capital of Terra del Fuego, he would ask, or how many pennies would you have to put on the top of St Paul's in order to reach the moon. I don't know, I'd say, thus enabling him to pass the answer on to me – and make room in his own brain for some other piece of newer, fresher information he was anxious to acquire. Why, when I have made love to you, do I talk so much?'

'I like listening.'

'Esther doesn't listen. Esther doesn't appreciate me. She doesn't appreciate me in bed or out of it. Then she makes a fuss because I don't make love to her. But it's not love she wants, it's her rights.'

He had never talked about Esther to her before. Susan felt encouraged. It seemed possible that at last a man was going to abandon wife, family, home and all for sheer love of her – and think his world well lost for sake of Susan Pierce. Then, and only then, she felt, could she begin to live. She began to apply paint and became so interested in the process she almost forgot all about him.

'She was most unsympathetic about my writing,' he went on. 'She didn't want me to write. She didn't want me to express myself. She didn't say much but she exuded hostility into the air. I would wonder what she did want from me. She has some money of her own, you know.'

'Is that why you married her?'

'Certainly not.' He was shocked. 'She was a very pretty, plump, messy, intelligent, cultivated girl from a good middle-class family. I don't know why she married me – my father was a non-commissioned officer in the Indian army; we had pretensions but no style. She had style but no pretensions. I thought myself very lucky. We were both at art school. We were both trying to escape from our backgrounds.'

'And did you?'

'I did. I don't know about Esther. There was too much money in her family. Anyone can escape from class. Money is a harder conditioning. I lived on hers for a time. She's never forgiven me. But why did she offer? She said I should stay at home and paint, and she'd pay the bills. I tried for a full year. And do you know what? I didn't paint a thing. We spent too much time drunk or in bed. The situation was too humiliating, you see, for either of us to be anything or anywhere else. It's a year I prefer to forget. Then Peter was born and I went into advertising and we settled down. Yet although now I earn a lot of money she still believes that it's she who keeps me. She believes this not with her mind but with her feelings. That initial outrage on her feminity was too great. Yet she insisted, she insisted, that I rape her finer feelings. Why? You are a woman, can you tell me?'

154

She felt so like crying at this simple statement of fact that she could not reply. He did not notice, but went on talking.

'I think that women are determined to suffer at the hands of men. They will manipulate every situation in the world to ensure that they are in the right and the man is in the wrong. Show me a wronged woman and I will show you a baffled man, who wants no more than to eat, sleep, make love and procreate, and can't understand what all the fuss is about. That's what I like about you.'

'What?' she asked in alarm.

'You don't suffer. Not really. You pretend to for the sake of appearances but you are more like a man at heart. You take your pleasures simply and your relationships lightly.'

'Then I am afraid,' she said, 'that you are a homosexual at heart.' She put down her brush and sat with her head in her hands.

'Don't get upset. I intended it as a compliment and it in no way offends me that you should level accusations of homo-sexuality at me, since it is so patently untrue. I am a simple, natural man, and you are very beautiful, and let us face it, very easy.'

'Why don't you just go home to your wife?'

'I shall, presently when I am ready. I have just noticed that pipe on the mantelpiece. Does William the poet smoke a pipe?'

'Yes.'

'What a pretty domestic picture it makes in its arty kind of way. William's on one side of the fire with his head full of words and you on the other with your head full of symbols. Uniting, no doubt, on the hearthrug from time to time. A pity you two don't have children. They might grow up to rule the world. But then of course William already has a wife, hasn't he, and prefers to have his children in wedlock. And I dare say maternity would slow you down in your headlong career through the marriages of other men.'

'You have no right to talk to me in such terms. I asked William to go the day I met you. What more do you want? What sort of person do you think I am?'

'An easy lay.' He spoke sullenly, and they were silent for a bit.

'I am glad you're jealous,' she said presently.

'I'm not jealous. Why should I be jealous? Just get that fucking pipe out of my sight. You shouldn't keep other people's phallic symbols on the mantelpiece.'

She broke the pipe in half and put it on the fire and they were happy, after a fashion, for a while.

'Is the bulb growing yet?' he asked. He had bought her an expensive lily as a present. They had planted it together in a pot with some potting compost. She watered it lovingly but it showed no sign of green. The dull earth remained flat and undisturbed.

'No.'

'I'm afraid you forget to water it.'

'I don't forget. I water it faithfully but nothing happens. I haven't got green fingers.'

'Neither have I. Esther has, or used to have. After she ran away she had the back garden concreted over. She said it was tidier.'

'Ran away?'

'Never mind. You can't hold against people the things they do when they're mad. I wish she hadn't done that to the garden. I like looking at flowers, even though they seem to wilt if I so much as touch them. Go on painting. I like to sit here while you paint. I wonder why Esther couldn't bear me to paint? She would never leave me alone. She was forever offering me cups of coffee and biscuits and delicious new dishes. It was hardly surprising I got nothing done. When I was writing my book I locked it away but I left the key where she could find it. I wonder if she looked? I would write more and more extreme things; things that I knew would annoy her more than anything, to try and provoke her into taking some notice, but I don't know whether she even looked. When it's published she'll have to take notice, won't she. She'll have to read it then. Other people will force her into it.'

'How could you bear to live all those years without love?'

'I never said I didn't love Esther,' he said in some alarm. 'I do. I always have. She's part of my life. She's Peter's mother.

The happiest time in my life was when Peter was a very little boy; we made our contacts with each other through him. A smile each to each above the tiny head – you know the sort of thing. But they were real smiles, you wouldn't know about that. Parenthood is a whole dimension of life which is meaningless to you.'

'You reproach me with having no children. But yet you wouldn't father a child on me. It's not fair.'

'Why do women always want things to be fair, I wonder. Nothing's fair. And I wasn't reproaching you, either. You have to be brave, mind you, to be a childless, husbandless woman. Women are only considered to exist through merit of their relationships. I admire you for being so brave.'

'It's very sad,' she said forlornly, 'that I should like and admire you so much as a person, and that you should like and admire me, I sometimes think, only as a female body. I thought for a time you were a serious kind of man, who could appreciate all of me and not just a bit of me. I don't want to be wrong about you. Don't make me be. You have been tied down in this hideous marriage of yours for so long I don't think you know what you're doing any more, or thinking, or saying, or feeling. I want to save you. I want to rescue you.'

'I don't want to discuss my marriage with you, Susan. Why do you insist? It will do you no good and only upset us both.'

'Because you've got to. You can't go on like this, living with someone who doesn't appreciate you. You need to be encouraged and loved and admired, and all your wife does is stultify

158

every natural wholesome feeling you've got, until you're so full of defences you're just not capable of feeling properly any more.'

'I don't know why you have such a high opinion of me. Esther, who knows me better, has a very different view. I am her tame, despicable ad-man.'

'But that's what she's tried to make you. She seeks to despise you.'

'And you don't?'

'No.'

'I wish I could believe it. I say terrible things to you sometimes. Why do you put up with it? Other women wouldn't.'

'You try to drive me away, I know, because then everything would be simple and easier for you. But it's not what you really want.'

'I want food,' he said. 'I want pie and chips and HP sauce, the kind of food we had when I was a little boy. I can't raise my sights above my stomach. I'm sorry. I know I should, but really I can't take anything seriously but food.'

'Stop trying to get out of it. You've got to make some kind of decision. It's important. It's the turning point of your life. Your last chance.'

'Come here,' he said, 'body.'

Laying her on the bed he turned her unclothed body this way and that, and pumped her limbs here and there, penetrating every likely orifice that offered itself to his view. He slapped and bit her, pulled her breasts and tore her hair. It afforded no pleasure at all and she suffered a mounting sense of shock and outrage. This was not what she had meant at all when she embarked upon her career of cheerful sexual freedom. She cried, which interested him, but he did not desist. She was half on the bed, half on the floor, while Alan paused, searching his memory for details of vaguely remembered adolescent reading, when William let himself into the room. They covered themselves, separately, with blankets, and Susan flung herself weeping into William's arms. He put her in a chair, unmoved, and stroked his neat beard.

'I left my pipe,' he said. 'Where is it?'

'I threw it away,' she said. 'I'm sorry. He made me. Oh William, make him go away. He's being so horrible to me.'

'Good,' he said. 'You had no right to get rid of my pipe. One way and another you are no better than an animal. I am sorry I disturbed you at your antics. Pray continue. I am just going.'

'Oh don't go away. Don't leave me with him. Why did you go away when I asked you to? I didn't really want you to. We were so happy together, weren't we? Please don't leave me. Not now.'

'You've never cared twopence for anyone in your entire life,' said William, 'and I'll tell you something else. You're a lousy painter. Go back to your ad-man. You deserve each other. I hope you take better care of his property than you did of mine.' He nodded to Alan. 'Good day.'

He left. Presently Alan laughed. Susan continued to weep.

'I'm sorry,' Alan said. 'But really I feel much better. You have a marvellous body, did you know?'

'I don't care about my body,' she said. 'What about me?'

'It's time you got married.'

She looked at him, instant hope mingling in her brain like instant coffee in boiling milk, but he shook his head at her and went back to his wife.

'Why do you bring me to life,' she cried out after him, 'if only to kill me again?'

'It's terrible to be used like a pound of butter,' said Susan to Brenda, 'because that's what he did. I won't go into details, you're too young, but he went all the way through the book of rules, bending me and him in every possible direction. What has love got to do with rules? Or positions?'

'If you want to be loved,' said Brenda piously, 'you have to love. If you had loved him enough you wouldn't have minded. You would have been glad to have afforded him some pleasure.'

'It wasn't anything to do with pleasure or with sex. It was just all his miserable rage and hatred coming out; he was humiliating me on purpose.'

'Do you think he's like that with his wife?'

'I am afraid not, with her no doubt he is more than reverent. That makes it worse. I was prepared to take him seriously and he was determined to treat me like a whore. If he had managed to have a decent relationship with me he might have been saved. Now he will have to be a dandruff shampoo man for the rest of his life. It's his loss, not mine. I learned about him in time. I shall never marry him. And it wasn't only what he did, it was what he said. In the morning his words were still all over me, like thorns.'


'You still haven't told me what made you leave Alan,' Phyllis was saying to Esther at about the same time. Nausea held Esther like a rapist's arms. She still ate, on the principle that she might as well give in and enjoy it, but the food in her mouth seemed offensive, and her very words tasted disagreeable. Phyllis stood at the stove stewing apples for her friend, having a vague notion that stewed apples had therapeutic powers. 'I can understand that when you go on a diet you would disturb all kinds of things you didn't know about, like shifting a heavy wardrobe and watching the little creatures scuffle away, and finding old beads and letters you'd forgotten about buried in the fluff. But wasn't being married to Alan something to cling to? I would have thought it was the one positive thing you had, being a wife. How could you ever know you were right to do such a thing?'

'I left Alan once before. That time it was easy. It was a positive act. I wanted sex, and life, and experience. I wanted things. I was young. I could hurt and destroy and not worry. I had excuses. This time it was different. I did it because the state I was in seemed intolerable, not because I hoped for anything better. And yes, it is true that this time I have been conscious of a sense of sin, not against Alan, but against the whole structure of society. It is a sin against Parent Teachers' Associations and the Stock Exchange and the Town Hall and Oxfam and the Mental Welfare Association and the Law Courts –'

'Do you feel sicker, Esther? Should I call the doctor?'

'No. I have lost my faith in doctors – it was a wilful sin against all those human organisations that stand between us and chaos, marriage being one of them. My mother was very shocked when she rang home and found me gone. She followed me down here.'

Esther's mother, Sylvia Susan, was small, neat, pretty and sixty-five. She was flirtatious, and wore clothes so up-to-date that people, never having seen anything like them before, would stare after her in the street. Now she wore a grey denim smock with matching kerchief in her hair. Her legs were thin and knotted. Esther was able to look at her own with something approaching approval. She sat at the table biting her fingernails, which was something she only did when in her mother's company.

'I wish you wouldn't worry me so,' said Sylvia. 'It is not fair of you. Am I not due for a little peace? Could I not be allowed, for once, the luxury of not worrying about you?'

163

'I am not worried about myself, so I see no reason for you to be worried.'

'Look at you! You're in a terrible state. You've got soup all down your front. You always were a messy child. I don't know who you got it from. It wasn't me. I did all I could to train you but you were very stubborn. You were too clever, that was the trouble. You could read when you were three, and type when you were four.'

'A pity it all came to nothing.'

'It made me uneasy at the time, and I was right. None of my side of the family had brains. You got them from your father. And your body became overgrown in its attempt to keep up with your brain. Your father would stimulate you, that was the trouble. He encouraged you to think when what you needed was the exact opposite.'

'I don't think you ever really gave the matter two thoughts, Mother, you were too busy.'

'I know you have this view of me as a frivolous party-going woman, goodness knows why. If I went to parties when you were a child it was simply to help your father. Giving parties was an expensive and tiring occupation. But his business depended on his social contacts.'

'You were good at those.'

'Now what do you mean? Esther, what is the matter with you? Come home with me. What you need is a rest, and some proper looking after and then you will go back to Alan. You are in one of your states, and it's no use taking any notice of the things you say or do. I shan't let them hurt me. I know you too well. You are my daughter, when all is said and done.'

'What is the matter, Mother? What is all this talk of daughter? Have you decided you are lonely, after all these years? I prefer it down here, thank you very much. And I am not going back to Alan.'

'Now, you are being ridiculous. Now listen, Esther. You remember the doctor you saw last time, who did you so much good –'

'I am not mad. I know you want to think I am, but I'm not. I had a nervous breakdown fifteen years ago, from which I am quite recovered. At least I suppose it was a nervous breakdown. That's what people said. It seems, in retrospect, more like a fit of sanity, from which happy state you and your doctors wrenched me, forcibly. By the time you'd drugged me and shocked me I was in no state to do anything but go back to Alan. Why should one necessarily be mad just because one prefers not to live with one's husband? I am not mad now.'

'No one is saying you are, darling, just overtired and overstrained. And I'm sorry, I know it's hard for you to admit it, but you were definitely off your head then, the last time. You had no reason for leaving Alan. You couldn't give one. He was earning good money, at last. Your marriage had got off to a shaky start, I can tell you now I cried nightly all that first year when he was living off you, sponging off you, but then all of a sudden he changed, and he was doing marvellously, and

165

we could all see what a wonderful future you both had. It was Peter's birth that did it, of course. It was all Alan needed, a sense of responsibility. I don't know why you had to go to that art school. You should have gone to the University and done something with your brain, since you had one, instead of hanging around with that extraordinary crowd. But by some miracle, which I will never understand, it all turned out all right in the end, until you suddenly take it into your head to walk out on your child and husband for no reason. If that's not madness, what is?'

'I could see where it would all end, that's all.'

'What do you mean?'

'Like this.'

'Like what? And, what has happened between you and Alan if it is more than just your neurosis? Is it another woman?'

'Yes and no.'

'I'm sorry dear, but it's yes or no. There are no half ways where these things are concerned.'

'I am afraid there are.'

'No doubt that's very modern of you. But let us try to get at the truth. Is he being unfaithful to you?'

'Mother, will you let me and Alan run our own marriage, or ruin it, as the case may be? I'm a grown girl now.'

'One would hardly think it. Look at it, this room. Look at the state you're living in! It's disgusting.'

'You didn't run your own life any too successfully.'

'Now what can you mean by that? I was a good wife and your father was a good husband. I am lonely now. You are all I have in the world. But he left me well provided for.'

'You never cared a fig for him. You went away on your holidays leaving him all alone with only me to look after him –'

'I was very delicate. I was never strong. What would you have me do? I'd have been no use to either of you if my health was broken.'

'And I used to dread you coming back and sneering at me, which is what you did, for being ugly and fat. But it was your fault that I was ugly and fat. And if I wasn't good at looking after Father, I was only a child, wasn't I? Or meant to be.'

'You should have aired the sheets. You were twelve. That's quite big. You knew sheets ought to be aired. It was damp sheets that gave him rheumatic fever. The doctor said so.'

'It's an old wives' tale about damp sheets and rheumatic fever. You held that over me for years. You ought to be ashamed of yourself.'

'And it was his weak heart after the rheumatic fever that killed him. I've never said it as plainly as that before but it's in my heart, and it ought to come out.'

'Don't you worry, it's been leaking out of your heart for the last fifteen years. I know what you think. But it's your own guilt speaking. Who were you off with on your medically recommended holidays in the South of France? Who? What were you doing, and who with? That's what killed father, not my damp sheets, but your adulterous ones.'

'You are out of your mind, Esther. Don't let's quarrel. We haven't quarrelled like this for years. If I'd had a son we wouldn't ever have quarrelled. Daughters are so possessive about their fathers, that's the trouble. I did what I could in the face of my own nature, which is the best any woman can do. But it's all in the past now. I am getting old. You seem young to me still, a child, but in the eyes of the world I suppose that even you are no longer young. You won't marry again, who would want you? You are too gross. You must stay married to Alan. I beg of you. You have some money of your own, but it is folly, folly, to throw away your security, and your status, and the respect the world accords you as a married woman and a mother, and your husband's income, and presently his pension, which will be generous. Three-quarters of his salary I understand.'

'Women of your generation seem to regard men as mealtickets. It's not very nice.'

'It's a great deal less painful than regarding them in any other way. And it is practical. Youth goes so quickly. It is such a short span in one's life. When it is over you recognise that comfort, status and money in the bank are really more important to a woman than anything else. And her family, of course. Esther, you are my family.'

❏

168

'The thing about my mother,' said Esther to Phyllis, 'is that she never thought anything was important except her bank balance in her entire life. This lover she had in the South of France gave her jewels and money. That was why she went to him, not for love. And my poor father died trying to keep up with her demands – her financial demands, not her sexual ones, she didn't have those. I don't understand how I came to be born, nor, I think, does she. He was such a gentle clever man. All he ever wanted to do was sit in his study reading old law reports, with me to dust and bring him coffee and cook his dinner, but she insisted. She insisted. She made him go out into the world and entertain clients and steer so near the edge of the law he lived in dread of falling over, and ending up in prison. I think prison would have been a relief to him, in fact. He could have been the librarian and pottered.'

'Did he like Alan?'

'He liked him at first, when Alan refused to keep me or make a home or do anything but paint. I think he admired him for being so strong. I liked Alan at that time, too, except that my mother went on and on about him using up all my money. Then Peter was born, anyway, and everything changed. And father became ill with his heart, because of the rheumatic fever and then he died, so I don't know what he was thinking, in the end. I had a feeling he turned against Alan when Alan went respectable and that's another reason I felt allowed, that time, to leave. This time I have no one's judgement but my own to go by. I used to be terrified I would end up like my mother. Many women do. They turn into their mothers far more easily than sons turn into their fathers.'

'You take these little holidays from your husband, all the same, the way your mother did from your father. Perhaps if you were seven stone lighter you would be more like her than you imagine.'

'Out of the mouths of babes and sucklings –'

'I am not as young as all that. I am thirty. That's a terrible age to be. There are wrinkles beginning to show around my eyes. And as for breast-feeding, it fills me with horror, the very thought of it. I don't want to be like a cow, with a baby draining away my strength. That's another reason I don't have a baby. I've never dared to tell anyone that before. Don't let Gerry know.'

'You can always give them bottles.'

'But that's not right. That's failure. Babies should be breast-fed. They force you to, in hospitals.'

'That is only the latest revenge of the doctors. A more subtle torment than just any old birth pains, which have too short a duration for their liking. You are right to fear maternity wards. Every resentment against the fecund female grows rampant there, like weeds, strangling commonsense and kindness. Any hospital is a place of myths and legends, and a maternity one is worst of all. When Peter was born bottles were considered more hygienic than dugs and breast-feeding a damaging habit; but then to compensate one was obliged to underfeed one's child, to keep it perpetually thin and pale and crying, if of course it was not too weak to cry at all. You must never pick your child up and cuddle it, was what they said then, that's spoiling, and interrupts its routine. But what

170

they meant was, you shall not enjoy this baby you have had the presumption to have. We shall never, ever, let you.'

'Peter's not thin and weak now. He's a well-built boy. He takes after his father.'

'I took no notice of them. I fed him when I wanted and when he wanted. We were happy. Then my father died. I have been in mourning ever since. He seemed more like Peter's father to me than Alan ever did.'

'You still have not told me why you left Alan. The apples are cooked. Will you try them?'

'Thank you. With sugar and cream. I begin to feel a little better. I hope Peter is all right. But why should he not be? He has his compensations, he does not need me. He is more like Alan than he thinks.'

'I think you should be worrying about your husband.'

'My husband is an attractive man. There will always be women to look after him. He will use them while it suits his purpose, then he will damage them and send them away.'

'He is not like that at all. You wrong him.'

'You seem very possessive of my husband, Phyllis, all of a sudden, and to know a great deal about him. Do you fancy him?'

'What a thing to say.'

'Because you're welcome.'

Phyllis blushed crimson and spilt the sugar.

Esther watched her sweeping up the elusive grains with pleasure.

'Your trousers are too tight,' Esther said, 'you're getting fat. Gerry won't like it. He likes his wives to be small and his women to be fat, like me.'

When Phyllis straightened up there was a look of despair on her face.

'You are awful,' she said, 'I just don't know what to think or what to feel any more. There aren't any rules left.'

'Calm down, and I'll go on with this story, which you so rashly wanted to hear. Peter came to visit me a couple of days ago. I was more pleased to see him than I was to see my mother.'

'Oh Mum,' said Peter. 'I wish you would come home. It is very upsetting. Just because I leave home, doesn't mean you have to too. It is very embarrassing explaining to people, and it's not very nice in this room, is it? Everything is usually so tidy at home, how can you bear to live like this? It makes me think you must be depressed. It is very worrying for me – I shouldn't be hindered with worries at my age. It is bad enough being captain of a cricket team, and having duties and responsibilities towards Stephanie, without having to feel responsible for a miserable mother, too. That should be Father's business. He's taken to cooking. Recipe books everywhere. "Hi there, Mrs Sussman I presume," I said to him the other day, when I was home for the weekend, "slaving away over a hot stove again I see," but he didn't think it was funny. He doesn't think anything is funny, nowadays. Oh Mum, come home. It is all so dreary like this.'

'But you have your own home now, Peter. Choose to use your former home as a weekend hotel, by all means, but kindly do not insist on cheerful chambermaids. Or indeed on resident ones. This is where I live. You live somewhere else. Your father lives in yet another place. How you and your father choose to behave is now entirely your affair. Thank God I am not around to witness it.'

'Mother, you begrudge me any sex life. It isn't fair.'

'I most certainly do not. Have it off with all and sundry, male, female, bald-headed as you will. The pair of you.'

'Dad behaved very foolishly, I know, but don't take it out on me. She is a female fatale, Mother. He couldn't help it. There are these women about, you know. Insatiable and irresistible. It was just bad luck he happened to encounter her when both your spirits were so low. You should never have stopped eating, either of you. In middle-age, food is far less troublesome than sex. There is something terrible, tragic, monumental, in thinking of Father with that beautiful, beautiful girl –'

'Have you seen her, then? Where? How?'

'She called to visit me. To apologise for breaking up my home.

173

I was trying to get on with my homework and waiting for Stephanie to come back from work when there was this knock at the door, and there she was. This vision. So unhappy, so distressed. I think there is a kind of kinship between us. She understands so much. She has so very, very much feeling. Women with feeling are very rare, Mother. But it is all over between them now. She has grown out of the stage of looking at older men. She prefers her own generation. That is maturity.'

'I see. What does Stephanie think about this?'

'One of the nice things about Stephanie is that she doesn't really think at all – after school it is such a relief, all this non-thinking. As a schoolboy one has to use one's brain all day; even playing cricket demands great mental concentration. I really do need you at home to talk to, you know. I am fairly grown up for my age but every now and then I become con-fused. If girls didn't like me I can see I would lead a narrower life, but it would be a more peaceful one, wouldn't it, and not so alarming. I mean, see how it confused Dad's life, simply fancying a girl as one could fancy a dish of strawberries and cream. Because that is how it was with Dad and her – he saw her as a symbol of delight, not a person. It was most distressing for her. Mother, somebody has to look after her. She is not good at looking after herself.'

'She's older than you. You're the one who needs looking after.'

'You are perfectly right,' he was triumphant. 'That is exactly what I have been trying to say. Oh Mother, come home.'

'There he was, you see,' said Esther to Phyllis, 'playing with fire and frightened of getting burned. All set for an affair with suburban Susan, coming to me to be protected from himself, hoping that my outrage would be strong enough to turn him back from the incestuous paths to which he had set his face. Going to bed with Daddy's mistress, it's far too near for comfort to going to bed with Daddy's wife. I used to fancy my mother's rich lover, I remember, being too scared to actually fancy my Dad. But now I refused to be outraged. I had given him the eighteen years a mother has to give a son. Now he was on his own. I wanted to save my outrage for myself. Not waste it on a child who had youth on his side to save him from the direr penalties of obsessive fornication. I was older than him, and needed my outrage if I was to escape my husband.'

'Perhaps your mother was right, Esther. Please try and think rationally about things. When you talk like this I get upset. Nothing is as I thought it was; you make my whole world rock. You should see a doctor. An old-fashioned, physical one, I mean. Things have gone too far with you. You can have your frontal lobes cut, do you know, and then you never worry about a thing. You're just happy all the time. All the time.'

'Poor Phyllis. Is that next for you? If cutting your breasts open and stuffing them doesn't work, try cutting open the brain? You don't half pursue happiness to extremes. You'll corner it somewhere, won't you. In a little dark corner of your coffin, I dare say, finally you'll corner happiness.'

'I assure you I am very happy. It is you I worry about, Esther. You shouldn't think of that lovely boy Peter in those terms,

175

much less reject his pleas for help. He wanted to be saved from Susan Pierce. It was your duty as a mother to save him. You should have packed and gone home there and then.'

'Well I didn't. If Alan doesn't ask me to return I never will. And even if he does, I won't. I have my pride. Did I tell you Susan Pierce has just been to see me? She brought me a flower pot.'

'What an odd thing to do.'

'It was a present Alan had given her. She said she couldn't make things grow, but she thought I could, and she couldn't bear to leave that lily to wither up and die. It was just an excuse to see me. It was as if she wanted the entire family. Not content with the father, and then the son, I really think she would have welcomed a Lesbian relationship with me.'

'Oh really Esther! She's no dyke. She's just sex-mad.'

'You mean I have been talking to you all this time and still see human relationships in terms of sex? It had nothing to do with sex. The sexual urge is concerned with the reproduction of the species. She just wanted to wriggle back, somehow, anyhow, into a family situation. That she chose a genital method of doing so was merely coincidental. She could have done it more simply by doing our charring for us. It was a great misfortune that Alan had his family pictures on his desk. It was me she had been reaching out for all the time. I realised it when she handed me that flower pot full of dried up earth. It was Mummy's and Daddy's bed she wanted to be in. She wanted to know what happened there. She wanted to be included in the mysteries. A pity that the mysteries, when at last discovered, should prove so trivial. A matter of plungings and positions. And yet the dark that shrouds all sexual intercourse, the dark of spirit and emotion, and the black cloak of love that makes one decent, leads one always to believe that there is something yet to be discovered. It is very aggravating, and responsible for a good deal of domestic confusion.'

'What are you talking about? You are a pagan. You are not decent. You are obscene!'

'Now what have I said to upset you so? I am telling you what you were curious about. About why Susan came to see me.'

'I felt so nervous about coming here' said Susan to Esther. 'But I thought I ought to try and explain things, and make them better. I wouldn't wish you to have hard feelings about me, or about your husband. He is an artist, you see. And artists are not like other people. The ordinary rules of morality do not apply to them.'

'Their immorality appears to me to be as dull and sordid as any ordinary persons. Alan is not, in fact, an artist, he is an advertising man, by profession, and by paucity of soul. That is to say he is talented, and intelligent, plausible and attractive, trivial to the bottom of his heart, and pathetic in his aspirations to a different way of life. That, however, is as may be. I may take a more jaundiced view of my husband, by virtue of my years with him, those chaste and temperate years, than you do by virtue of the couple of weeks, and the varied and various shaggings which no doubt you have shared with him.'

'You are not,' said Susan, sitting down, 'what I expected at all. For a wife you are very vocal.'

'I am sure it is most admirable of you, to come visiting to explain things to me. People ought to do it more often. What a coming and going there would be, week in, week out. What a knocking on doors, day and night, up and down the land. But there'd never be a woman at home when the knock came. She'd be out on the town herself – explaining.'

'You are taking advantage of me. I have been very upset by your husband.'

'Well don't come complaining to me.'

'And I am afraid he is unhappy, and it is my fault. And you are unhappy, and it is my fault. And Peter is unhappy because you two aren't together. It is very upsetting for him. Please Mrs Sussman, go home to your husband. We have all behaved so badly, I know. But there is only one person who can put things right, and that is you, by going home.'

'I would like to make something clear. My leaving Alan is nothing to do with you. You are welcome to him, I promise you. Anyone is. And probably are. When Alan embarked on this manic association with you, he was in a sad psychic state. You were a symptom, not a cause. A chicken-pox spot, if you like, but not the virus. You itched him, so he scratched. Now the spots have subsided, but the virus, I am afraid, remains. It is the unhappiness and discontent attendant on having too much leisure, too much choice, too little pain. And none of it is anything to do with you. Kindly stop indulging yourself, and go away.'

178

'You are making things very difficult for me. It is not easy, I know, for a non-artist, like yourself, to understand and forgive. It must all seem strange to you, if you cannot comprehend the suddenness, the awfulness, of love when it strikes. The helplessness which overcomes one, the misery when it all goes wrong, when one offers so much and is turned away.'

Her face had changed. She looked younger and uglier. She cried. Esther began to feel more kindly towards her. 'Mrs Sussman, he didn't want me at all. He wanted you.'

'He didn't have to want either of us, did he. He might have wanted the moon, or the Pope or the Queen. I am afraid the intensity of your rivalry with me prevented you from noticing anything of the kind. This knowledge might, perhaps, make you feel better. It is not that I have vanquished you. It is that we have both been wounded in a battle which we should never have embarked upon because it didn't concern us at all. People will make sex an excuse for anything. What is it that you are carrying in your hand and watering, so sweetly, with your tears?'

'A present.'

'A pot of earth. For me? How delightful.'

'Don't laugh at me. It is not a pot of earth it is a pot plant. There is a lily down there. Alan gave it to me.'

'How sweet!' Esther peered at it elaborately. 'Alan's and your baby, as it were. It's not very advanced for its age though, is it?'

179

'Stop being so nasty. You were being nice before. I wish we could be friends. There is so much I don't know about things, and the more that happens to me the less I know. I only want to love someone and be loved back. Nothing I do goes right, it's like the lily. It won't grow for me. That's why I brought it to you. I thought you could make it grow. Something has to come out of all this. It must. If only a bloody pot plant.'

'Peter quite fancies you.'

A look of horror appeared on Susan's face.

'You know about that? I don't know how it happened, I really don't.'

'He wants to look after you.'

'Does he really? You don't mind?'

'Stop behaving like a little girl. You go all to pieces in the face of your elders, don't you. You become infantile at once. If I was you I should go and throw yourself at Peter's mercy and ask him to explain everything. He has a very neat version of the world, my son, far placider and tidier than mine. You can sop up his little boy helplessness when the dregs of it trickle out of his ears. And he can sop up your little girlishness when it flows and pours out of your every orifice. Play at mummies and daddies and daughters and sons in every conceivable combination you can imagine, but just leave me in peace.'

'I had no idea you were so clever. I wish my mother had been like you.'

Esther heaved herself out of her chair and turned Susan out, first snatching the flower-pot. She watered it tenderly with lukewarm water from a milk bottle, and sang it a little lullaby. But the earth didn't stir.

'That terrible woman,' said Susan, ungratefully, to Brenda. 'She's more or less pushing me into bed with her son. Any decent woman would have been shocked and scandalised at the very idea. She is very, very odd. No wonder Alan looked elsewhere.'

'Perhaps,' said Brenda, 'she wanted to be revenged on Alan. I mean to say, what an uncomfortable position for him. Supposing you and Peter got married. You having a former lover for a father-in-law. He a mistress for a daughter-in-law, and everyone knowing.'

'It would all be rather cosy,' said Susan. 'And companionable. I think I should like that. I'll walk down with you to the pub, and while you lie in wait for that silent man I'll go and call on Peter. It's Wednesday, and crop-haired Stephanie has a boy-friend she visits on Wednesdays.'

'What are those bruises on your neck?' Phyllis asked Esther. Esther, having told Phyllis about Susan's visit, had been violently sick into the lavatory. She returned to lie upon her bed, and opened her collar so that the old yellowing bruises on her neck could be seen.

'It's where Alan tried to strangle me.'

'He didn't. He never did!'

Phyllis put her hands to her own neck, grateful for a lucky escape. 'I am sure Gerry would never try to strangle me. I am sure he wouldn't. How did he try to strangle you?'

'He put his hands around my neck and he pressed and he squeezed and he tried to kill me. To put an end to me altogether. As if that would have solved his problems. I think, mind you, that I would strangle me if I was him. It must be a fearful thing to be a man and have a wife. Never to be able to do what you want without feeling guilty. Always feeling in the wrong, because wives are always in the right. I feel quite sorry for men sometimes.'

'But to try and strangle you!'

'I did call him an impotent old man. An impotent balding old man.'

'Perhaps you were angry.'

'But you see, it was the truth. He was spiritually impotent, totally, and physically impotent, partially. Once I had told him the truth, I had to go. There could be nothing left between us. Lies are never dangerous, not by comparison with the truth.'

'Esther, Esther,' cried Alan on the evening of the final day of the diet, 'I've lost another pound!' The weighing machine now

182

had a permanent position in the living-room. It was eleven o'clock at night, and the diet ended at twelve. Alan was in his dressing-gown, which now had an appreciably greater overlap than before.

'Esther, Esther!' he called in the direction of the kitchen, but no one answered. 'Another pound. Think of that! Of course I've been taking a lot of exercise. I'm sure that helps. But twelve whole pounds.'

There came a small rustling furtive noise from the kitchen. He leapt from the scales so that the dial swung wildly, and flung the kitchen door open. Esther crouched in a corner, like a woman taken in adultery. She was eating a biscuit. Rage overwhelmed Alan.

'You cheat,' he cried. 'You cheat! You're eating.'

'You're the one who cheats,' she hissed. She seemed half mad. 'You always cheat me.'

'What are you talking about?' He tried to snatch the biscuit from her. She resisted.

'Please,' she begged, 'please let me keep it. It's nearly midnight. The whole nightmare is nearly over. I must eat it. I must.'

He got hold of the biscuit and threw it to the other side of the room.

'You take everything,' she said. 'You take everything, and give me nothing. You take my life and you throw it away.'

'You're mad. You're mad again. They never really cured you, did they.'

'You made me mad.'

'You have no self-control. You are despicable. You can't even stop eating for a couple of weeks. You have to nibble, and cheat, and go behind my back, and lie, and twist, and cheat, and cheat, and cheat again.'

'I have nothing else to do but eat. What else have I got? You give me nothing. No love, no affection, no sex, nothing.'

'Take a look at yourself. You are disgusting. What do you expect?'

'I have given you everything. All my years, all my life. Everything I ever had all wasted. Every bit of love I ever had I gave to you. And now you just throw me away.'

'Like an old glove?' he enquired. She raised her hand as if to strike him, but he dodged. 'Oh calm down,' he said. 'All this fuss about an old biscuit. You're hysterical. Why do I always end up with hysterical women?'

'Is Susan hysterical too, then?'

'Here we go again. What is it you want, Esther? Why can't you be satisfied? You've got a home, and a child, and security, and a husband who comes home every night. I support you. I'm polite to you. I don't beat you. You're luckier than almost every other woman in the world.'

'I'll tell you my discontent. It's this. I think that if you found me ill and lying in the gutter you wouldn't bother to pick me up and take me home, you'd just pass by.'

'You're a fair weight to pick up. Ha-ha.'

'You can't resist being funny at other people's expense, can you? How they must hate you at the office.'

'Oh, cut yourself a slice of cake. I'm going to get dressed and go out.' He moved towards the door. Esther moved to intercept him.

'Where?'

'That is none of your business.'

Esther stood with her back against the door, barring his way.

'Where, I asked.'

'Where I want. Anywhere in this world to get away from you. You make me sick. You want to keep me in prison. I can't even go to bed when I want any more, because I hear your prissy little voice calling down the stairs like some teenager.' He mimicked her soft voice, '"Oh Alan, Alan, beddy-byes". What sort of life do you think I have, sitting in a bloody office day after day, getting nowhere, doing nothing, with only "Alan, beddy-byes" at the end of it? This is the only life I'm going to have. I'll be dead soon. And you make me live like this. I was born a *man*, and now look at me. I am scarcely human any more. I tell you, the day I married you was the end of my life. You squeezed my talents out of me. You depleted me utterly with your demands and your naggings, you turned me into a poor grey dried up company man with an income and pension. It's not me, and it's your fault. I hate you. You've cheated me of my freedom, and my life. You've stolen it.'

'You're a poor balding impotent old man. A dirty old man. I read what you wrote. All your sexual fantasies. You'd be mad to think anyone would publish them. They were the sick ravings of a lunatic.'

'You're the lunatic, not me. I don't *want* you in bed. How could I?'

'I despise you too much. I pity you.'

'Get out of my way.' He tried to push past her.

'No. Where are you going? To your Susan?'

'Yes. Are you surprised? You have driven me to it. You have played your cards all wrong. Mrs Sussman.'

'Perhaps you haven't played your cards so well either. Perhaps I have somewhere to go too. Men don't think of that. Do you think I just sit quietly at home, and take what you deal out to me?'

'What do you mean?' But a bland self-satisfied smile just crossed Esther's face and vanished again. 'What do you mean? Who would want you? Who in the world would want you?'

'You must be feeling very guilty,' said Esther, 'to assume my guilt when I haven't said a thing. Not a thing.'

'You fat slut.' He tried to move her from the door, but she spread her arms against it as if crucified. Noiselessly, they struggled. He was stronger than she, for all her size, and it was evident that he would get the door open in time, but she would not give in. Her face kept appearing, almost wilfully, in the path of his fists. He slapped her hand on the side of her face, and she tore at his cheeks, with her nails. He put his hands around her neck and squeezed. When she sank to the floor he let go. He opened the door and left the kitchen. Esther, still crouching on the floor, heard him go up to the bedroom, dress, collect his coat, come down the stairs and let himself out of the front door. Presently she raised her head and surveyed the kitchen. She stood up, ran a finger along a dusty ledge and cursed Juliet. She took a couple of biscuits, and poured some milk into a pan, and started to make herself cocoa.


'The night she walked out on him,' said Susan to Brenda in the pub, 'he came to see me. He'd never been in the night before, only in office lunch hours and on the way home after work. I didn't let him in. I didn't want to be treated like that again; like an old dustbin for all his old rubbish. And anyway I kept thinking William might turn up – isn't that your silent friend coming in?'

Brenda blushed and lowered her eyes. The man from the night before saw her, looked surprised, and then, gratified, crossed to sit beside her. Susan rose. 'I'll be off then,' she said, 'to see Peter. Make sure he buys your drinks, and not the other way round.'

'I can't speak to him, so I can't make him do anything. I'll just have to accept him as he is, won't I.'

'Put your charges up. Then he'll value you more.'

'I do live a very dull life,' said Phyllis to Esther. 'Gerry never tries to strangle me, and his girlfriends never come to visit me. Perhaps he doesn't have as many as he would like to think; perhaps in fact it *is* all talk with him –' she looked hopefully at Esther, but Esther made no sign of either assent or dissent – 'or perhaps it's just all over so soon they never get round to finding out my address. I think as soon as he gets what he wants he loses all interest.'

'That's right,' said Esther. 'It's in, out, and off. That's Gerry. Very boring, and not worth discussing.'

Phyllis fell silent. Then she ate a biscuit.

'Funny thing,' said Esther. 'I don't feel hungry any more. I think your horrible doctor was right. I was sickening myself. Now I'm purged, and I'm better. Eat up, Phyllis, it will do you good. You know the thing that disconcerted me most about Susan's visit? It was the way she called me Mrs Sussman, but Alan by his Christian name. I realised how small a part of his life I was, or ever had been. It was hard to stomach.'

'What are you going to do next?'

'Nothing. Stay here. Eat, read books. Die. Be buried. Rot. Be finished.'

'That's silly.'

'It is true,' said Esther. 'I am finished. I am over. It is very simple, really. I am a woman and so I am an animal. All women are animals. They have no control over themselves. They feel compelled to have children — there is no merit in it, there is no cause for self-congratulation, it is blind instinct. When I was a girl I searched for a man to father my children. My eye lighted on Alan. I had my child. Now the child is grown up and I have no further need of the man. I shuffle him off. And he has no need of me, because women age faster than men, and I am no longer a fit mother for his possible children. Let him beget more if he can, and start the whole thing over again with someone else. That's his affair, not mine. The drive is finished in me. I am dried up. I am useless. I am a burden. I wait to die. Phyllis, I am making myself feel hungry again.'

'I am not an animal.'

'You coward. You prissy miss, with your curls and your sexy little suits. You're an animal. You said to me once you were chained to your bed. Well so you are. Because you're a female animal, and your brain and your mind and all your fine feelings are no help to you at all. You're just a female animal body, fit to bear children and then be thrown away. And if you don't have children, you'll be on the rubbish heap all the sooner, and being stamped on like an empty milk carton to boot. So watch it.'

'You're still not well.'

'I don't expect to be well.'

189

'There's someone coming down the steps,' said Phyllis, who was sitting near the window. She craned her head upwards. 'Oh good heavens, it's Alan. It's your husband.' She turned to her friend, panic-stricken, and trembling.

'Don't get so panicky,' said Esther. 'I know all about you and him.'

'How? What do you mean?'

'It has been evident from your manner all day. It doesn't matter in the least. I doubt that either of you enjoyed it. A simple matter of tit for tat. And you can think about *that* phrase a little longer, and repeat it to your bosom doctor, from me.' She crossed to the door to let her husband in. He loomed crossly through the doorway.

'What are *you* doing here?' he said to Phyllis. 'What mischief are you making now?'

'Esther is very ill,' said Phyllis. 'She needs help. I'm glad you've come – she says the oddest things.'

'What are you playing at, Esther? It's absurd, living in two places at once. I thought you'd come to your senses sooner and come home. Your behaviour is very inconvenient for everyone. Have you calmed down enough to come home, do you think?'

'I don't want you down here, nagging, go away. You're a pompous old bore.'

'Peter needs you. He's very upset these days. He's emotionally immature. He's unstable.'

190

'I think he'll be all right.'

'It's you he needs.'

'I have needs too, you know.'

'My face is beginning to heal, at last. It has been most embarrassing. It went septic. Your nails must have been dirty.'

'Oh you poor thing,' said his wife.

'You really must try not to be so hysterical. It does a lot of damage. You can't go on living in this pigsty. How much do they charge you?'

'Five pounds a week.'

'It's robbery. It's damp. It's a slum. I haven't seen anything like this since I was a child.'

'We lived in a room like this the first year we were married.'

'And a terrible place it was, I remember. You've got fatter, you don't look at all well.'

'I'm back to where I was before I started that terrible diet of yours.'

'I was on it too,' said Alan.

'Is that an apology?'

'What have I got to apologise for? Let's just forget it all. Come home, Esther, don't be silly.'

'I like it here. No one nags. I can breathe better too, now the swelling on my throat has gone down.'

'Throat?'

'Where you tried to strangle me.'

'You drove me to it. You goaded me.'

'I'd better be going,' said Phyllis brightly.

'Oh don't,' cried Esther falsely. 'Do stay to tea, Phyllis darling. You'd love her to stay to tea, wouldn't you, Alan?'

'And you can stop that here and now,' he said. 'If you walk out on me you can take the consequences.'

'What about Susan?'

'What about her?'

'I was with you then. I had done nothing wrong.'

'I was on a diet. I was very upset. There was all that terrible business with the agent and the publishers. It was very humiliating for me, Esther, and you didn't help at all. Susan was a nothing.'

'Poor Susan then. Just a nothing. I think she will be revenged.'

'How?'

'Never mind. That's another story. I will tell it one day.'

'Wives always win in the end,' said Phyllis hopefully; she had moved into profile against the light, so that her new and improved breasts stood out to advantage. It was for Alan's benefit but he took no notice. 'All they have to do is hold out long enough.'

'You silly prissy smarmy common bitch,' said Esther. 'I don't think I can stand you much longer, Phyllis. Will you please take yourself and your bosom away, and this nagging bore of a man with you?'

'But it's true,' Phyllis persisted, with a note of hysteria in her voice. 'Wives win.'

'And what a victory, over what.'

'Please will you both calm down,' said Alan. 'There is no point in you staying here wasting money. You can't be happy here. You might as well be at home where you can be of some use.'

Esther put her head in her hands. She appeared to be defeated.

'No,' she said, 'we mustn't waste money, I suppose I might as well be there as here. It doesn't seem to make much difference where one is.'

Phyllis began to grizzle.

'Oh shut up Phyllis,' said Alan. 'Why do you keep butting in on other people's family quarrels? I hope you haven't got much luggage, Esther, I only brought the Mini.'

'Just what I took with me. A few old clothes. I'll leave the paperbacks. And that stupid pot plant. We'll leave that.'

'The plant is growing,' said Phyllis. 'Can I have it?' Esther got up, crossed to the window sill and peered into the flower pot. A little sprig of green disturbed the dusty surface. She was inordinately pleased.

'Good heavens! Do you mean to say I did that? Do you mean to say it's growing for me? Alan, look!'

But Alan did not turn round. He was looking with amazement into the food cupboards.

She shrugged.


On the other side of London Susan cried happily into Peter's shoulder and recited tales of domestic living with William and sexual adventures with Alan, while Peter lovingly blancoed his cricket pads. And in the pub Brenda held hands with the man she couldn't speak to, and was overwhelmed with such a sweet surge of love and gratitude that tears came into her eyes. He wiped them away, gently, with his very white pocket handkerchief thinking she had been drinking too much and that he must take her home quickly in case she fell asleep.